THE LIE THAT HAD TO BE

THE LIE THAT HAD TO BE

Sharon Gibson Palermo

Thistledown Press Ltd.

Canadian Cataloguing in Publication Data

Palermo, Sharon G., 1947 –
The lie that had to be

ISBN 1-895449-44-8
1. Italian Canadians – Atlantic Provinces –
Fiction.* 2. World War, 1939-1945 – Evacuation of civilians – Canada –
Fiction. I. Title
PS8581.A487L5 1995   C813'.54   C95-920055-X
PR9199.3.P348L5 1995

Book design by A.M. Forrie
Typeset by Thistledown Press Ltd.
Printed and bound in Canada

Thistledown Press Ltd.
633 Main Street
Saskatoon, Saskatchewan
S7H 0J8

Thistledown Press gratefully acknowledges the financial assistance
of the Canada Council for the Arts, the Saskatchewan Arts Board,
and the Government of Canada through the Book Publishing
Industry Development Program for its publishing program.

To those who have suffered in war
and
to my Italian relatives, without whom this story would
never have been imagined.

I wish to thank Tim Wynne-Jones whose suggestions
contributed much to the vibrancy of this text and
Glynis Ross who generously shared her knowledge of
Whitney Pier. I wish to thank them both for their
time and their faith.

There are no quotations, but research is from Kenneth
Bagnell, *Canadese, Portrait of the Italian Canadians*,
(Macmillan Canada, 1989) and "Italian
Canadian Detainees" (Sunday Morning, CBC Radio,
January 21, 1990).

Contents

 *Preface*

It is 1940. Rennie Trani is a ten year old girl living in an area of Sydney, Nova Scotia, known as Whitney Pier. There is a war on, and the names of the enemy —Hitler, Mussolini, Germany —are on the radio and in the adults' conversations constantly. But the war is far across the sea and doesn't touch Rennie. At least, it doesn't touch her until the late afternoon of Monday, June 10. . . .

Tyrants, Toads and
Paper Dolls

R*obbie!*" Rennie felt her quills rise up. She had known her brother was up to something. Why else would he have to pee just after Mama told her to wash out the bathroom sink? Now the sink glared up at her, green muck from rim to rim, the peppermint smell of toothpaste attacking her nostrils like dragons. She glared back at it and then at her brother, standing at the door, grinning like a gorilla. *You wait!* She ran her fingers into the toothpaste, catching it beneath her nails, and smeared it across his cheek.

Toad! You're such an ugly little toad! She could see his brown warts sprouting.

"Aagh!" Robbie screeched. Suddenly Papa was there, the tyrant king, standing over them with his arms across his wide chest. Rennie's delicious feeling fell.

"Look what he did, Papa." Maybe Papa would see that Robbie was a toad. Maybe he would hug her and she'd let her prickles down. His black eyes followed her pointing finger to the sink. His thick eyebrows drew together. He laid a deep frown on Robbie and then on Rennie.

He didn't hug her. Everything about him was hard, even the Italian words that came from his mouth. "Look at what *you* did."

"I *had* to. He was mean on purpose." Her voice quivered.

"I expect you two to be good to each other. You are brother and sister. You will need each other for your whole lives. Now, Roberto, go in the kitchen and wash your face. Renata, get this sink cleaned up fast. Don't be late for school." He turned and followed Robbie toward the kitchen, but Rennie's protest, "Robbie should do it," brought him back.

"I want to see that sink sparkle, signorina."

Rennie squinched her face hard and turned away to hide the hot, hateful tears which threatened her eyes. She turned on the cold tap and spread the water around until most of the sliminess disappeared down the drain. She could feel Papa behind her, his arms across his chest again, making sure she did it right. Why couldn't she turn *him* into a toad? Why couldn't she be a witch with long black nails that waved evil spells at his face? The tears came now, burning her cheeks. She poured cleaner on a cloth and rubbed it around. Her nose was running from crying, but she still wanted to sneeze out the pine scent. She washed everything down the sink, and then dried it with a fresh cloth, her hand shaking. Papa was still there. She rubbed away every drop of water. Now could she turn around? *How?*

Her shoulders closed together and her eyes glued themselves to the floor. She turned. Papa stopped her from leaving. He put his hand under her chin and lifted her face. Her cheeks were still wet and she couldn't look up.

"You're older, Renata."

Please stop, Papa.

"Now, are you going to go to school with your quills up?"

That was their joke and the tease meant he forgave her. Still, she was afraid to look at him. She tucked her forehead into his chest and then wrapped her arms around him. He pressed her close so she could hardly breathe. He smelled just like her good papa.

She felt a little better walking to school alone. How much she loved Papa, and how she hated it when he was angry with her. Sometimes she thought he *liked* her grumpiness. It was he who had first called her a porcupine.

And it was true. A person needed quills against tyrant kings and tormenting toads. Her parents must have known that when they named her. Rennie was more like a porcupine's name than a girl's.

It wasn't fair. Everyone else in her family had names that were OK in English. Riccardo was Rick. Sergio was Serge. Loretta was Loretta and that was beautiful. Roberto was Robbie. But *Rennie* sounded short and squat and babyish, and that's what people thought of her, too.

She thrust her hands into the big floppy pockets of her sweater. It was a white cardigan, warm and loose, with wide ribbed cuffs and bottom. It closed her in completely with lots of room to spare and the pockets could hold *anything*, nearly her whole arm, if she pushed down far enough. It was really Rick's sweater, but he'd given it to her because she'd been so unhappy when he went away to university last September.

"Hey, Rennie!" Julie ran up to her on the school ground. "How come you're so late?"

Rennie smiled. Julie always understood when grownups were unfair, so she told the story, the true parts, not the dream parts, and how it was all Robbie's fault. "But you just wait. He'll be in big trouble first chance I get."

"Good! Hey! After school, let's go to my house. I've got brand new paper dolls. You'll love them, Ren!" The girls skipped to the line up and stood still as angels while the nuns patrolled the ranks making sure all children's heads were facing straight ahead.

At Julie's, Mrs. McLean peered through the kitchen door and warned them to be careful of the house. The girls started upstairs.

"What does she mean?" asked Rennie. What could they do to it?

"I bet she's been cleaning all day. It's Daddy's birthday." Julie didn't seem to think anything was strange, but Mr. McLean would never care how neat his house was. He was always messing things up to have pillow fights and tugs-of-war with Julie and her. He probably wouldn't even notice how messy Mrs. McLean looked.

Oh, well. Mama said Mrs. McLean was the quiet type. Quiet wasn't exactly right. Gloomy seemed more like it.

She hadn't cleaned Julie's room. It looked as if Julie had been playing cards on her bed that morning and left them there. Her pajamas were thrown across the floor and her dresser was cluttered with 5 and Dime jewelry and play lipstick. Julie shoved some of this aside to make room for her sweater. Then she danced out into the middle of the room and, her blue eyes flashing, waved her arm into the air. From her wrist dangled a loose silver bracelet with a plaque that said "Thomas McLean" in strong Roman print. She plopped onto the bed beside Rennie and caressed the bracelet all over.

"It's so wonderful. It reminds me everyday of the proud, brave thing Tom's doing. I'm keeping it safe for him, and you know what, I think it's helping me keep *him* safe, too."

"That's stupid." Rennie was fed up with hearing about Julie's brother. "You can't keep him safe just by wearing his I.D. bracelet."

"It seems like I can. And, I really do think I can, too." Julie straightened her back and turned the name plaque toward her face. It caught some sun from the window and glistened.

Rennie let out a long, disgusted sigh. "Show me your paper dolls."

"I will. But first, you have to admit that Tom's braver than Rick. And he's saving our country for freedom and Rick isn't."

"I'm going home then." Rennie could feel her skin start to pinch. Rick cared about freedom too, but he had won a scholarship to Saint Francis Xavier University and he was going to be a doctor. That was just as important as being a soldier. Besides that, Papa said that Tom wasn't fighting in any battles. The soldiers were just waiting in England until they were needed.

Anyway, the whole war was far across the sea and had nothing to do with her except that the grownups talked about it a lot and made kitchen conversations *so* boring.

She stood up, but Julie had been moving around her room and straightening her bed. Her bracelet was on her dresser and she had her paper dolls out. "I'm only joking. You don't have to admit it," she said.

Rennie didn't know what to do. Julie *did* believe that Tom was better than Rick, but still, she had those nice paper dolls that they hadn't even touched yet.

She sat on the edge of the bed and leaned against the dresser. She kept her sweater on. It was fuzzy on her arms and held a comforting soap smell. This was the first she'd worn it in almost a week, since it took a few days to dry after washing. There was always an argument when Mama wanted to wash it. Rennie needed to feel as close to Rick as

Julie did to Tom. And besides, she needed warmth. Even though it was June 10, it was still chilly outside.

Julie laid the paper dolls out on the bed. There was a soldier, tall and square shouldered, with four brass buttons down the front that would shine if they were real. There was also a teenage girl whose head came to his shoulder. Her waist was pinched in tiny and she had wavy blond hair to match his blond crew cut. The soldier seemed a lot like Tom McLean, and the girl could be Julie a few years older because they were both skinny and very different from Rennie. Her own hair was short and dark and she had solid bones, according to Mama, and a firm cushion of flesh that was nicely squeezable.

Julie seemed to have forgotten about Tom and Rick. She plopped herself down at the end of the bed with her legs folded in front of her and studied the dolls. "Who do you want?" she asked.

"Who do you?"

"You're the guest. You choose."

"OK. The teenager. We can trade later, if you want." Julie handed over the teenage girl. Julie was nice. Rennie pulled her legs onto the bed. She opened her sweater so that it flopped widely at the sides. The girls started to play, walking the dolls toward each other. This was a trench in the war, with soldiers, and loneliness. The Tom McLean doll was sad. The teenager would go to war with him. She could cut her hair short and they could be heroes together, and maybe die together. "Come on. We'll draw a uniform for her," suggested Julie, but Mrs. McLean called up the stairs for them to come down.

"Bring your sweaters," she said.

Now what? It had been a good game.

Julie swept her sweater off the table. Rennie followed her.

In the Crystal Clear Glass

Downstairs, Mrs. McLean stood with an ear to the radio, nuzzling her cat. She looked brighter in a fresh black and white dress, but the girls' entrance seemed to startle her. She flicked off the radio, and, frowning, sent them to the bakery. "We need a pie for your father's birthday. And, Rennie, by the time you're done, it will be time to go home."

It will? The clock said just after four, but Mrs. McLean had used a no nonsense tone. There was nothing Rennie could do.

The bakery window was filled with tall wedding cakes topped by miniature brides and grooms with pinpoint eyes and mouths. The girls bent down to pick their favourites, then discovered themselves in the crystal clear glass. Julie shoved her elbow into Rennie. "Porcupine!" she laughed, stretching her fingers out from the sides of her head like quills.

"Ostrich!" Rennie placed her hands around her neck and pushed upwards as if to stretch it. They stood up to compare themselves: a tall thin one and a slightly round medium sized one. Whoever heard of a porcupine being friends with an ostrich?

They went inside. *"Buon giorno, Julia e Renata!"* Papa greeted them in Italian.

"Buon giorno!" All of Rennie's friends liked Papa. Italian words seemed to bounce from his tongue. The bakery set him laughing. As for Rennie, it often made her smile to hear him speak English.

"What I can do for you?" he placed his floury fists on his white apron so he stood looking like a little baker man in a book of nursery rhymes —kind of fat, kind of short, kind of jaunty with his elbows out. "You come to learn to make bread? I beg Renata to learn about bread for so long, but no, that is man's work, she say." He winked at Julie and she laughed.

Rennie grinned and looked him straight in the eye. "It *is* men's work."

Papa was a baker. The sweet smells of the shop, the dough and pies and cookies, followed him everywhere. No one else should do that work or carry those smells. Certainly not *her*. She couldn't. Papa was a magic bread maker. Everyone in town said so.

"Such crazy talk! *E pazza!* Yes?" Papa exclaimed, pointing his last question at Julie.

"No, Signor Trani. You're the bread maker. Mummy says so."

"Ah! And what is it your good mama would like for tonight, Signorina Julia?"

"It's a special night, *Signore*. It's Daddy's birthday and Mummy would like a pie if you have one."

"Yes, my Riccardo, he make good chocolate cream pies early in the morning." Rick was helping Papa in the bakery for the summer, starting the bread at 5:00 in the morning so Papa could sleep until 7:00. "Your daddy, he like chocolate cream, yes?"

"That's fine, *Signore*."

Papa boxed and tied up the pie, then pointed a playful finger at the girls, ordering them to wait. He went to the back room and returned with a bottle shape wrapped in brown paper and string. He stuck it inside another bag. "A little present for your daddy, his birthday. Tell him it my best. Grapes stomped by my own Renata and Roberto. And you don't take it out of the bag! No good for people to see young girls with a bottle of wine!"

"Papa! It *is* no good!" Rennie prickled. Sometimes she *hated* how he spoke English And did he have to mention grape stomping?

"Oh, you! So smart! Go now. My customers come."

So Rennie walked to the door and held it open for Julie. Julie had turned the wine bottle sideways and was somehow balancing the pie box on top of it. Did Papa *have* to give her wine? What if they met some nuns from school, with their awful black headpieces and eyes that saw everything? Papa should know better.

She and Julie walked past the shops of the main street in Whitney Pier. There wasn't much to look at. A doctor's office, a dress shop, a shoemaker, a pharmacy, a grocery. Down the hill, on the harbour side of the street, the long, hideous steel mill burped clouds of red dust into the sky. You weren't allowed to complain, though. Half the men in town worked there.

How lucky Papa was a baker. Most of the other men worked in the coal mines. Julie's father was one. He came home covered in black coal dust every night and had to bathe before supper. Rennie's sixteen year old brother, Serge, worked there, too, even though Mama and Papa had forbidden him to quit school. But he had insisted on either mining or soldiering, and there'd been arguments, loud and painful

and late into the night, until finally Mama and Papa gave in
to the mines. They wanted him happy, they said, but he was
too young to be a soldier. Rennie couldn't understand how
he enjoyed that gritty coal dust on him, but at least there was
quiet at night and smiling at the supper table again.

"What did your father mean about you and Robbie stomping the grapes?"

"He was only joking." It was not something to share with
the non-Italian kids —September wine-making. You washed
your feet really, really well and rinsed off the soap with about
a hundred rinses. Then you got into a big pail and stomped
the juice out of the grapes until your legs turned purple six
or seven inches up! It was the only time ever that you could
really get messy. It was a family festival. But the others
would think it was *horrible*.

"No, he wasn't. You really *do* stomp grapes. My mother
told me."

"Then why did you ask?" Rennie accused.

"Oh, ugh!" Julie shivered and tried to push her shoulders
back from the bottle. "How can my father drink this? You
stepped on it!"

"Then give it back!" Papa loved his wine. Why should he
give it to people like that?

"No! It's a gift!" Now Julie hugged the bottle with one
arm, making certain not to tip the pie with the other. Rennie
wanted to yell at her, *How could a coal miner worry about dirt?*,
but she didn't. Coal miners were important people in Whitney
Pier. She jammed her hands onto her hips while she and Julie
glared at each other. Then she turned away and headed
toward the bakery.

Maybe she'd stop and complain to Papa. He would understand. *But*, that wouldn't be the end of it. "Now tell me all

the things you like about her," he would say, and then he would make her try to list them. There were lots of things she liked about Julie, but . . . just then Robbie came charging around the corner on his bicycle. He nearly hit her, but he switched and swerved, right in front of a pickup truck. It screeched to a halt and Robbie rode off.

"Stupid girl!" he shouted as he went.

"You'll be sorry for that!" Rennie screamed, breaking into a run for the bakery.

But as she came close, she slowed down to a walk. Coming toward her were Sergeant MacPhee and another RCMP officer that she didn't know. Rennie was sometimes friendly with Sgt. MacPhee's daughter, Maxie, even though she went to the Protestant school. They lived at opposite ends of the same street and in the summer they met each other rollerskating on the sidewalk. If Sgt. MacPhee were home, he'd come out to referee races for them and hand out chocolate.

At the door of the bakery, the officers stopped. Sgt. MacPhee hesitated a moment, watching Rennie come toward them. Missing his usual smile, he opened his mouth as if to say something, but then changed his mind. The officers went into the bakery. Rennie had a funny feeling about it. Papa supplied fresh bread and pastries for everyone in Whitney Pier. Townsfolk were in and out of the shop all day long, even police officers. So, why did her stomach feel so jittery?

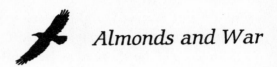 *Almonds and War*

The nutty smell of baking almonds greeted Rennie as she followed the officers into the bakery. *Mmmm.*

Papa was behind the counter closing a sale with Mrs. Hobinsky. The policemen moved off to one side and stood tall in their dark blue uniforms. Rennie watched everyone from the middle of the room. Papa gave her a wink and everything seemed fine. She wrinkled her nose at him, then he bent behind the counter in that secret way he had and came up with some amaretti, his wonderful almond cookies. He reached one to Rennie and tucked the others into Mrs. Hobinsky's bag next to her rolls. "Those — special for Alberto," he said. Mrs. Hobinsky took them out, laughing, "No, no! There is no need!" Even when she laughed, Mrs. Hobinsky looked and sounded serious. She had a husky voice and a straight up and down body with skirts that wrapped around her like tubes.

Papa's hand sprang up. *"Va bene!"* he said, which everyone knew meant "think nothing of it." He was in a playful mood. Rennie would ruin that if she told on Robbie, but still, Robbie wasn't allowed to ride his bike like a wild monkey. She started to munch her cookie. What did the police want?

Papa had leaned his hands on the counter top to smile at the officers. "What I may do for you?"

Rennie stopped chewing. A deep silence fell between the policemen. Rennie thought she heard Sgt. MacPhee clear his throat. "Mr. Trani," he said, "this is Officer Harnish."

"It pleases me to meet you." Papa held out his hand.

Officer Harnish kept his hand at his side. His shoulders seemed rounded though he stood straight. "Are you Cosimo Trani?"

"Why, you know I am." Papa smiled at Sgt. MacPhee, a slight question in his voice.

"Were you born in Italy in 1896?" continued Harnish.

Slowly, Papa, his eyebrows knitting together, stood up straight and stepped back from the counter. "That is correct." He used his clearest English accent. Rennie's own eyes began to squint into a frown. She finished her chew and swallowed.

Officer Harnish darted his eyes around the bakery, then walked to a bright white wall where a map of Italy, the British flag, and a picture of the Pope were tacked all in a row like colourful stamps of identity. He ripped down the map and the picture, crumpled them in his hand and tossed them to the floor. "Come with us," he ordered.

Papa's eyes widened and his jaw tightened, but he stood frozen, staring at the officers and shaking his head. Mrs. Hobinsky had been silent too long. She stepped to the counter and faced the officers.

"What's this man done?" she demanded.

Sgt. MacPhee wiped a troubled frown from his face and looked at her. "Mussolini has joined up with Hitler. We are at war with Italy."

What had that to do with Papa? Sgt. MacPhee spoke as if everyone would know, and it seemed that Mrs. Hobinsky did. She darted her eyes from the police to Papa and back again.

"But Cose is a Canadian now! He's a good, well-liked man in this town! For twenty years he's baked our bread. You know he's done nothing wrong, Angus!" She scolded like an angry mother. Rennie was standing by herself near the end of the counter. Her arms tightened at her sides.

Sgt. MacPhee's lips were grim and his knuckles seemed white around the policeman's cap he clutched in front of him. He pushed himself taller. Rennie shivered. He planted a steady gaze on Papa and said in a quiet but serious voice, "You must come with us."

Papa's playfulness had vanished, not in anger at Robbie, but in something that made his lips quiver and his eyes seem to melt. He came from behind the counter. For some reason, Rennie noticed how clean the bakery was: how the glass of the counters was completely spotless; how every cake platter and cookie tray was lined with a crisp paper doily; how the red, black and white floor tiles were perfectly square and held together with pure white lines of grout. She watched Papa remove his apron. It, too, shone white. He reached his arm around her shoulder and drew her to him. She threw her arms around his waist and looked up at him. "Papa, what are they going to do?"

"It's all right," he assured her.

"But what's wrong?"

"Not one little thing." For a second time that day he pressed her head to his chest. "There's some mistake." He lifted up her chin and looked at her with the same eyes as the tyrant king's, except they were softer. He told her he loved her, *"Ti amo."* She held on to him to keep him safe.

Sgt. MacPhee interrupted them. "Your wife can send clothes to the police station."

Rennie had never seen such a look on Papa's face. "There is a mistake," he repeated, pulling gently away from her and fumbling in his pants pocket. He took out his key and gave it to Rennie. He took her hand in his large and cushiony one and squeezed it until it tingled. "Lock up," he told her, and he left with the officers. They walked on either side of him, reaching the sky in their smart clothes. He was between them, short and plain, but with his silvery hair glistening and his head up. Rennie could barely turn to lock the door.

When she did, her hands shook. Somehow, she steered the key into the keyhole. Mrs. Hobinsky double checked the lock for her, then Rennie dropped the key in her pocket. It made an unsettling clink that she didn't expect. She stood for a moment, not knowing what to do.

"I'll come home with you, Rennie." Mrs. Hobinsky tucked the strap of her purse into her elbow and held the bag of rolls close to her. She gave the other hand to Rennie.

They hurried along.

There was Papa's frightened face. There he was going out the door between the two policemen.

She tightened her grip on Mrs. Hobinsky. "Rotten stuff! Rotten stuff!" Mrs. Hobinsky exclaimed now and then. The dust covered buildings of Whitney Pier seemed to pass them by trance like.

She threw her arms around Papa from behind and he became invisible. The policemen kept going.

She hadn't kept Papa safe.

At home, they went straight to the kitchen. Mama stood by the stove in the ruffled green apron Loretta and Rennie had made her for Christmas. Loretta, at the table, leaned over a comic book, but she jumped right up and pulled out a chair for Mrs. Hobinsky.

Mama was always ready to welcome a guest. "Helen, sit. I make you a coffee?" She pushed a strand of dark hair from her plump cheek and gave the sauce one more stir.

Mrs. Hobinsky refused the coffee and kept standing. She explained all that had happened.

"No." Mama didn't believe it at first, but, seeing the truth in Mrs. Hobinsky's eyes, she groped for a chair and sat down. The spoon sank in her lap. It left a dark spot that would spoil the apron forever. Rennie wanted to run to her, but her legs wouldn't move. Loretta did instead.

"But why?" asked Mama when she could speak again. "Cosimo love Canada. And I need to send clothes? Where will they take him?" But there was nothing more that Mrs. Hobinsky could tell her. She jumped up and began making decisions. *"Mie figlie,"* she ordered her daughters in Italian, *"il pranzo.* Have supper ready for Sergio. *E dove Roberto?* His papa will smash him! He never tells me where he goes!" She ran upstairs to collect Papa's clothes. When she came down again, she spoke to Loretta. "When Riccardo comes in, you send him to the station. He can explain to the police." Before she left, she turned to Helen Hobinsky. "Thank you, thank you," she said in English.

Mrs. Hobinsky grabbed her hands. "I've done nothing, Caterina, but I'll stay here with the girls. When Robbie comes in, I'll send him for Albert. We'll sit with you."

Mama was gone. Rennie's hands were cold. Loretta was crying — fourteen years old and weeping like a baby. Rennie grabbed the dishes and cutlery for the table. She counted enough for the entire family, including Papa and Mr. and Mrs. Hobinsky, and placed them around loudly, ordering Loretta to move her elbows. Loretta snapped at her, "Leave me alone! You don't even feel bad! Don't you love

Papa?" Rennie bit her lip and ran upstairs. She would not cry. She *would not* cry. Everything was going to be fine. Hadn't Mama said Papa would be home?

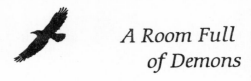

A Room Full
of Demons

Rick and Mama came home without Papa. Mama's face was puffy, and fresh tears fell at the sight of her four other children whom she gathered into her arms, somehow making certain to give each his or her own personal squeeze. Then she drew a handkerchief from her pocket and wiped her eyes as she led them into the kitchen and slumped into a chair.

Loretta sat next to her again and nestled herself into her arms. Robbie, the Hobinskys and Serge sat or stood in various places while Rennie leaned against the hard wooden frame of the doorway. Rick stood just inside it with his hands in his pockets. He looked from one questioning face to another and answered them with a despondent shrug. Serge handed him a glass of wine and he sat down at one end of the table. The darkness of his hair and eyes and skin, which normally shone handsomely, now seemed to turn down the light in the whole room. His speechlessness was painful and Rennie was unable to take her eyes from him.

Finally, Serge said, "Well? How long are you going to make us wait?"

"Hey. We'd better stay calm. No one wants to keep you in the dark." Serge's face had a look of great impatience, but Rick went on before he could say anything more. "They

wouldn't listen to me. They said they know all about Papa.
I don't know what they meant by that. I *know* they know all
about Papa —and it's nothing to arrest him for. But, they're
taking him away and they wouldn't say where. It's not just
him. It's Frank, too, and several others from up in Dominion.
They're all down at the station."

"Frank Da Vita! What will happen to his lumber yard?
And what will Luisa do with those two little babies? Who'll
feed them?" Mrs. Hobinsky was horrified.

"Not Papa, that's sure," said Serge. There'd been many
times Papa had arranged for the Italian Club to collect money
and food for the families of men who were sick or out of
work.

It was 8:00 and still light outside, but the kitchen was
taking on the dull gray of the dusk. Robbie, sitting next to
Rick at the table, gazed up at him with his mouth half open.

"Are they hurting him?" he wanted to know.

"No. The men are all just sitting there at the station. They
had a good supper. They're not in jail or anything."

Rennie was trying to fight the terrible tightness in her
throat. Mrs. Hobinsky put food around, giving her a nudge
to help. That was good. Better to move than stand like a stone,
aching.

They ate pitifully little, then sat around. Many Italian
families, including the Da Vitas, lived at the Trani's end of
the street and around the neighbouring corners. They, and
other good friends as well, were in and out, comforting,
exclaiming and crying. Rennie found a chair near the corner
of the kitchen where she could listen but not be noticed. She
felt she had goose bumps all up and down her arms even
though she still wore Rick's warm sweater. She pressed and

folded the sleeves close to her arms, trying to make them fit her more snugly.

The sounds seemed to sink into her. Mama and Loretta, wrapped in each other's arms, never stopped weeping. Luisa Da Vita cried, too, as she rocked her infant and let her whimpering two year old squeeze between her legs. In deep voices the men spoke of Mussolini and *Italia*, dear *Italia!* What would happen now? The other women were up and down, running water for coffee, washing up cups, comforting always. "You must be strong, Caterina, Luisa. We must all be strong. We must help each other."

And why? Why? All evening everyone kept crying why? Because Papa was president of the club, and Da Vita, too, was a leader in it. Because they kept the idea of Italy alive. Because they spread care in the community.

"But those are good things," Loretta protested through sniffles.

Mama shook her head. "There is a war." She was sitting heavily, her hands holding one of Loretta's in her lap.

It was too confusing. Rennie stayed quiet, nothing to say, nothing to ask. Robbie, too, hadn't spoken since supper. She fixed her eyes on him from across the room. Papa was gone and there was Robbie. Hateful. *Hateful toad. I'm rubbing toothpaste in your hair. Oh, yummy, green and gooey all over! Papa will get you. He'll give you a licking and lock your bicycle in the shed for a month!*

But it was *she* who had angered Papa that morning and it was her badness he would remember, not Robbie's.

She realized she was biting her nails and she stuck her hands deep in the pockets of the sweater. Her fingers touched a piece of metal. The key, she thought, and pulled it out. Rick would need it when he went to the bakery in the morning.

But instead of the key, she pulled out Tom McLean's I.D. bracelet!

Amazed, she held it in her lap and turned it over and over, admiring its shininess. It had been on Julie's table right next to where she had been sitting, but how had it come to be in her pocket?

The links nestled coolly in her hand, settling into the shape of her palm like a small, tame snake. The words "Thomas McLean" shone up at her. She stared at it — Tom, the soldier — and suddenly the snake turned mean. She glowered and shoved the bracelet back in her pocket.

Across the kitchen, the radio droned ominously. Cigarette smoke circled the air like the tails of genies set free. Its smell mingled with the smell of strong coffee, but there was no magic.

Serge hadn't sat since supper. He paced the floor, back and forth to the window, flicking cigarette ashes out the back door, running his fingers across the top of his head as if looking for a swatch of hair long enough to grab. There wasn't one and, finally, in frustration, he shouted, "There must be hundreds of Italian boys in the army and now they're arresting their fathers! I'm so glad I decided not to join up!"

At that, Mama jumped from her seat. "*You* decided?" she accused, breaking her gloom. The two stared at each other from across the table: Serge, the muscles beneath his shirt sleeve looking hard; Mama, her rounded arms and bosom, normally so comfortable, now strong in their fierceness.

Rick tried to help. "Ma, he was only talking."

"Only talking!" Her hand knifed the air, her words bit. "And *you*? What are you going to do now? Back to school in

September, yes? And me here to run the bakery alone, or close it down! Then how will we eat?"

"Mama, Papa will be home long before then."

"You don't know! No one knows, do they?" She broke into fresh sobs and Loretta took her hand to sit down again. Others in the room began to soothe each other with low mumbles.

A few tears came to Rennie's eyes. Her fingers had gone back to her mouth and the image of genies had faded. Mrs. Hobinsky warmed some milk, gave it to Robbie and her, and told them to go to bed. They had school tomorrow. From opposite ends of the room, they each sipped it down slowly, but neither went to bed.

At 11:00, Rick and Serge hushed everyone and turned up the radio. The Prime Minister was about to speak. There was silence around the kitchen. Rennie rested her eyes on Mama's fat ceramic pig which she kept on the counter. It was pink with fancy blue spots and it had a hole in its back where Mama kept nickles and dimes for rainy day spending. A "rainy day," she'd explained, was a day when there was nothing serious or important going on. From the radio came a voice, hard and sombre: Italy has entered the war on the side of Hitler. Canada is at war with Italy. All Italian men who are thought to be suspicious will be interned.

"*Suspicious?* Who has Cosi ever hurt?" Mama was near tears again.

Now, looking at that dumb pig made Rennie want to cry. *Everything* was serious.

She walked to where Rick was sitting and let him put his arm around her waist. Almost too frightened to hear the answer, she asked, "What does 'interned' mean?"

"It means 'put in prison'." His eyes met hers. Through their sadness they seemed to say, don't worry, but her heart beat faster and her hands went clammy. Papa behind bars like a bad man!

"Italian traitors!" someone shouted from the front yard. "Down with Italy!" Rennie jumped. She looked toward Rick again, but suddenly everyone was up and rushing toward the sound. She and Rick followed. An egg smashed against the window and oozed its insides down the glass.

"Who was that?" cried Luisa Da Vita.

"They're gone!" Serge banged his hand on the window frame. The sound thudded through the room. He opened his mouth to utter an oath, but he caught Rennie's eye and changed his mind. "There are little kids in this house!" he said instead.

Mama walked to the window and looked out. Others moved away as if to give her space, but Rennie pushed herself into her arms, finding a welcoming spot. It was good to be there all alone, wrapped in the big soft cushion that was Mama.

The Smells of Supper

Everyone had trouble falling asleep, but Serge and Rick went to work in the morning. Mama opened the door to Loretta and Rennie's bedroom at 9:00. She told them to do the housework later. She was off to the bakery.

Rennie tossed in her bed as pictures of Papa and Serge and Sgt. MacPhee crowded her head. She should have gone to school to be with friends. She *would* go in the afternoon, after the dinner dishes were put away and the house was swept and dusted. She got up to do the dusting early. Loretta wouldn't appreciate it, but no matter how angry Loretta, or anyone else, made her, she was going to be nice. Papa deserved it.

She eased her cloth over the windowsills and tabletops of the downstairs rooms. She had to rinse it out many times, washing yesterday's collection of red dust from the mill down the drain, but she didn't mind. She had the whole morning in which to do an especially good job.

She let the water splash through her cloth, swirling the red around. She soaked the cloth again and held it in a clump, squeezing pink drops in running polka dots around the rim of the sink. Each dot was a little person going somewhere — to the drain — was it a prison or an army camp or school where her friends would be?

Serge stormed in. He stomped muddy boots into the kitchen and pounded his miner's hat onto the table. "Where's Ma?" His eyes were wild. He was red and sweaty and he had a bruise on one cheek. He was home far too early and there wasn't a speck of coal dust on him.

"At the bakery." She waited for him to say more, but he turned to leave again. Loretta came running down the stairs.

"Serge! What happened?"

"They won't let us into the mines!"

"They won't let who in?"

"The Italians! I'm going to the bakery," and he was gone.

Loretta and Rennie sat at the table and stared at each other. Loretta had a terrible look on her face. "Oh, Ren," she cried, but when Rennie just kept staring at her, she said, "Don't you understand?"

"No." *Please don't make fun of me.*

"It means Serge won't be able to work. And we're going to need his money now. Mama said people will stop coming to the bakery."

"Why?"

"*Rennie . . .*" Rennie's face tightened up, but Loretta's turned sad and she ran around the table to hug her sister. "Oh, poor baby!" she said. "You're just a baby, aren't you?"

Rennie's prickles went up. She pushed herself away and ran out the front door, something screaming inside her. In no time, she was across the small patch of grass that was her yard, and onto the sidewalk.

She walked rapidly down the street, staring at the pavement ahead of her, pushing back her furious tears. There were a few people out, mostly mothers and grandmothers with babies and small children, strolling along or standing at the edge of lawns to gossip, but she never looked up. She walked and walked, up and down street after street, barely noticing the trees and fences which streamed past.

Everything was wrong and there was nowhere to go.

It might feel good to watch the harbour water sway back and forth, but she couldn't get there easily. The monstrous steel mill building blocked the way and though she might sneak through the fence or around it somehow, she'd surely be chased away by workers.

The rest of the town was houses and shops. There was only her own backyard and she finally went there and sat in the corner where the slanty door to the basement met the blue boards of the house. A scraggly evergreen bush rose next to her on the other side. She curled her knees up tightly and pressed herself close to the house as if in a tent. She was as hidden as possible.

Why were people mean to her — Loretta and Robbie and Julie and even Papa?

She put her chin on her knees and looked out toward the vegetable garden where Papa worked each evening until it was too dark to see. A low shelf of greenery had poked through the earth. There was a row of tomato plants. It was slightly higher than the other rows because Papa had grown them inside for weeks before putting them out. Tomatoes were his favourite and he wanted lots of them, firm and ripe, before the frost came. Who would take care of it now? Would they be able to grow the food they would need for fall and winter?

Why was Papa gone? What had he done?

And why was Serge angry and? . . .

I can fix it all. Just walk straight into the police station and tell Sgt. MacPhee, in a clear, strong voice, that Papa is good. . . .

A gray mist fuzzed the colours and edges of the garden plants. She slid to the ground and fell asleep against the hard concrete of the house, the bush casting a thin shadow over her eyes. When she awoke, the light had changed. The sun streamed in from a low angle, making her blink. She started into the house by the kitchen door. It must be time to help Loretta get the noon meal ready and then go off to school. She felt excited about going to school. It seemed a year since she'd seen her friends. Julie would be so happy when she returned the I.D. bracelet.

But inside there were supper smells, not dinner smells: spicy tomato sauce, fried potatoes and boiled beans. And where *was* everyone? She let the door click shut. Robbie came charging in from the front room.

"You're getting the switch! Mama said she can give it as good as Papa can." Her heart jumped in fear. What had she done?

Behind him hurried Signora Da Vita jostling her baby in her arms, the toddler clutching her skirt and scampering to keep up. She thrust the baby over to one hip, sat down, and pulled Rennie to her. Wildly, she caressed Rennie's hair, looking into her eyes as if she'd been gone forever.

"Renata! Don't you know the worries we have? Where have you been?"

"In the backyard," said Rennie meekly. She was beginning to understand. "I guess I fell asleep. I didn't sleep all night."

"Oh, *mama mia!* You poor baby! Caterina is frantic! She's looking all over town for you — and Loretta and your brothers are, too!" She pulled Rennie tightly into her. Rennie was tired of all these hugs, but at least it was kindness.

The front door shot open and Mama's frightened voice called out. "Luisa? Roberto?" Rennie bit her lip though she hadn't done anything wrong. Besides, Mama never hit her children. If she thought it was necessary, she left it to Papa.

But Papa was gone.

"In here, Caterina." Immediately at seeing her daughter, Mama's face relaxed. She threw her arms around Rennie while wet tears covered her cheeks. "Thank God you are safe!" She smothered Rennie in kisses, then straightened up and wiped at her face. She took a deep breath and began scolding excitedly. "Renata, you have given us a terrible fright! Loretta had to do all your work today and now it is nearly 7:00! None of us have had our supper because of you."

In a rush, Rennie explained the whole day — how angry she'd been with Loretta — how everything was terrible — and why was Papa gone? Suddenly, Mama hugged her again.

"We must get along with each other," she blurted out, "and you two," she told Rennie and Robbie, as if it had been on her mind, "must look after the garden —*with no fighting*. We must make Papa proud." It was all she could say before she sat down and cried. Rennie stood in front of her, watching. *Could* she make Papa proud? *Could* she keep from fighting with Robbie — or Loretta, or Julie?

"But why did they take Papa?"

"Because," said Serge, who had just come in, "they think Papa wants our country to lose the war. Everyone in town hates us."

Mama shot around to face him. "No! Everyone does *not* hate us!"

For the first time in Rennie's life, everything — and everyone — seemed wrong. No one knew what would happen tomorrow.

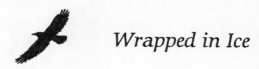

Wrapped in Ice

After supper Rennie was desperate to go to Julie's house, but she was not allowed, so she went to the living room and sat on the sofa in her angry pose, with her legs folded up and her arms crossed in front of her chest. But even before she sat down, her anger had faded. Mama had some good reason for refusing to let her go.

In a while, Mama sat beside her, her eyes as dark as night and gentle as a summer day. "You look like you lost everything, . . ." she said.

"I have to see Julie." Rennie's explanation sounded weak even to herself.

"Not tonight." Mama didn't want to speak, but she had to. "Julie's father is a miner and there are hard feelings. Her mother had some nasty things to say today."

"Like what?"

"Never mind," said Mama, "but I think you would be sent home. You and Roberto can come with me to the Scioppa's to play with Anna and Giorgio. Signor Scioppa is another miner who couldn't work today. Things might be rough for a while and we're going to have to be especially good to our friends."

"How?" asked Rennie. It had never occurred to her that they weren't good to their friends. In fact, everyone in

Whitney Pier had always understood when others were in trouble, so how could the McLeans turn her away? She and Julie spent every afternoon together.

Still, the funny feeling she had about Mrs. McLean was real. She remembered yesterday when she'd had to leave at 4:00.

But Julie *needed* her bracelet! If she didn't get it tonight, that would be two whole nights she'd be without it.

Obediently, but unhappily, Rennie went with Robbie and Mama to Anna's house. Anna was a good friend.

"You should've been in school, Rennie. It was awful," she said as soon as they arrived in the front yard. "No one will play with us anymore. All the other kids hate the Italians now. In our class, it's just you and me and Pietra who'll play together."

"Julie will be my friend."

"No, she won't. She's one of the meanest. She said she hates you. She said you lied to her about stomping grapes and you were selfish with her paper dolls. She said she'll never speak to you again. She said all of us are liars."

Rennie felt as if a large ball were rolling up inside her chest to her throat. Again, she pressed her arms across her stomach, as if she could stop it.

"It's not true," she insisted, when she could speak. Julie wouldn't tell such lies. And just because Mr. and Mrs. McLean were angry, it didn't mean Julie would be.

"It is true. But look, we got each other. We've gotta stick together, Mama said."

The ball in Rennie's throat had disappeared. The familiar prickliness had taken its place. Anna was there wanting to play, but how could she? She walked around to the back of the house and Anna didn't follow her.

She sat on the back step where the last glow of sunlight squinted at her through the trees. She rounded her back toward her knees like a porcupine and imagined the quills sticking up.

No one could touch her — not Julie or Anna.

She wondered if Julie could've said those things, but if she had, she'd change her mind as soon as she got the bracelet back. In fact, maybe that's what she was so mad about — losing the bracelet — and she was taking it out on Rennie. Like Mama might explain about Robbie. He'd get in trouble with Papa or some neighbour would holler at him to stop riding across their lawn, and then he'd be mean to Rennie. It wasn't fair, but it would get better when Julie was happier.

What if Julie thought she stole the bracelet? But no. She would have told Anna that.

Rennie straightened up and let the sun shine on her face.

Anna and Robbie and Giorgio came running to the back. "Come on, Rennie," Anna called to her. "We're going to play war. It's starting to get dark and spooky out. Giorgio's the general."

Giorgio, the oldest, thrust a stick machine gun into her hand. She took it easily and fell into line, as if being a soldier would get the anger out.

"Hup, two, private!" Giorgio ordered, "off to get the Germans!" With the guns over their shoulders, they fell in line next to him and marched across the yard. At a signal from Giorgio, they were all down on one knee shooting at the bushes.

"Kill the German devils!" Giorgio ordered. "Bbbbbbbbbbbbbbbbbb!" their machine guns fired. Then, suddenly, Giorgio shouted "Retreat!" and they jumped up and charged past the house and toward the street. There they caught their breaths and were ready to march again.

"Aircraft bombers!" shouted Giorgio and they transformed into roaring jets zipping around the house in zigzag fashion. Then — "Under siege!" — and they dropped behind bushes, defending their land with their stick artillary.

Finally, it was truly dark and the children flopped to the ground by the picket fence in the front of the house. Rennie stretched out full on her back. The big white moon and the cool, moist air enchanted her. It was the Night Fairy.

"Good battle, everyone!" Anna commended them.

"Yup!" said Robbie. He aimed his machine gun at Rennie, "Bbbbbbbbbbbbbbbbbb!" then he rolled over on the grass laughing.

"That's it, kill each other," someone scolded. It was Mr. McLean tramping down the sidewalk. "Better than killing us Canadians."

In the dark, Rennie couldn't see his face, but such a comment had to be a joke. Cheerfully, she said, "Hi, Mr. McLean. We're shooting the Germans."

Mr. McLean moved close to her. "Of all people, you should know the Italians are *with* the Germans, not against them!"

"But we're *Canadian* Italian, Mr. McLean," Giorgio tried to explain.

Mr. McLean narrowed his eyes and looked the children over. "Huh!" He turned and marched on.

The children looked at each other in dismay.

"See?" said Anna.

Rennie didn't answer but wrapped her arms around her knees and stared past everyone. By the light of the street lamps, she watched Mr. McLean's balding head bob rapidly into the distance. She heard Giorgio explaining to Robbie what people thought of the Italians now. But they were all wrong. "We're loyal citizens, just like them."

Rennie felt slightly reassured by "loyal citizens", whatever that meant. She reached down and ripped out some blades of grass. They were smooth and cool — comforting. It was obvious Julie must not understand about the Italians.

Later, as Rennie sat on her bed in her nightgown, she smiled at the I.D. bracelet in her hand. It was the most important thing in the world to Julie and when she got it back, she'd know that Rennie, and all her family, were as good as they had always been.

Mama came in. Sadness was carving its place on her face. Rennie wiped the smile off her own and explained about the bracelet and about how Julie thought Rick should be a soldier.

"Probably Julia has changed her mind by now," Mama said.

"Why?"

"Renata, Riccardo is going to be a doctor. He's going to help people get well, not kill them. That is the best thing anyone can do for Canada. Did you say a prayer for Papa?"

"Yes."

"That's good. That's all you should worry about. Only Papa. Now, goodnight." She kissed Rennie and tucked in the blanket, but not with her usual attentiveness. She seemed to be pulling away, wanting to leave the room.

But Rennie didn't pay much attention to that. She just wished Mama had told her what was probably true: that Julie wouldn't want Rick to be a soldier because he was Italian and, now, Italians were the enemy. But tomorrow, *she* would not be the enemy.

She went to sleep right away. When she woke up, she washed carefully and put on a clean dress. Then she put on

Rick's sweater so she could show Julie how the bracelet must have fallen into its very wide pocket.

She ate her breakfast quickly and washed out the bathroom sink, making it sparkle.

She kissed Mama goodbye and ran to school. Anna and Pietra were waiting for her, but she went straight to Julie.

"Julie, guess what I've got!"

Julie pretended not to see her. She thrust her chin out and turned away. Rennie moved around to get in front of her, but Julie kept turning until she had a clear path ahead of her.

Rennie tried to keep up. "It's something you'll want!"

Julie stopped and turned to her. "You're a rotten Italian and we all hate you!" Her eyes seemed to glow witch red. She marched away.

Rennie stood perfectly still. She felt wrapped in ice. She put her hand in her pocket and clenched the bracelet. "You're mine now, pretty silver bracelet," she said.

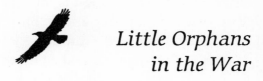 *Little Orphans in the War*

The bracelet would not leave her alone. All that day, Rennie's hand kept sneaking into her pocket. She knew she had to keep it safe and she had to keep it quiet, but it was getting in her way. She couldn't think about anything else — not for one minute. Deliberately, she'd pull out her hand and say, under her breath, "Don't touch!" but as soon as her mind went to her school work, back went her hand to the bracelet. She fiddled with the links during multiplication; she slipped it around her hand when reading. She rubbed the smooth joints where the links fit together; she knew how beautiful the bracelet was and how noisy it could be, — and ugly, too, and mean — like Julie — like Tom.

No one could call it stealing.

Could they?

No. It had simply fallen into her pocket. And *why?* Maybe she was *supposed* to have it. It was hateful. It was a soldier's bracelet — a soldier in a country that hated her father. It didn't deserve to be seen. It didn't deserve to be! *Maybe* she had a job to do.

Maybe she had to get rid of it. But how? It was unbreakable, and hiding it wouldn't destroy it. Besides, there wasn't a place in the house that Mama or Loretta didn't dust or clean out regularly. She would need to think about this.

When she arrived home from school, there was bread and milk on the table for her. Mama greeted her quietly, too much like Mrs. McLean. Rennie dug into her bread, complaining out loud that it didn't have butter. Butter was expensive, Mama said. They'd be doing without.

Rennie ate and wondered about the bracelet. Once, Robbie had flushed Papa's watch down the toilet. He'd borrowed it and lost it, and when he'd finally discovered it, he was too scared to admit it. He thought the toilet would take care of it, but it came back and settled at the bottom. Someone else found it, and Robbie got a licking.

"When you're done," Mama interrupted her thoughts, "you should weed the garden."

Rennie went upstairs to put on play clothes. She closed the door and laid the bracelet on her bed, as if looking at it would give her an idea. It shone silver bright, like a cold moon, on her blue bedspread.

This was like war, she realized. What did people do in war? For one thing, they burned buildings. In the cabinet, above the kitchen sink, were matches.

Rennie stuck the bracelet in the pocket of her shorts where it lay heavily. She snuck the matches and went out back. Crouching in a duck walk, she dug a little hole in the dirt with her fingers, close enough to the house so she couldn't be seen from a window, but not close enough to endanger the house. She made sure there were no old leaves or grass near by.

She brushed the dirt from her hands and pulled out the bracelet. She placed it in the hole. Everything trembled — her thighs, her hands. When she tried to strike the match, it bent. So did the next one, and they both fell by the bracelet.

Her lip hurt from biting it. *Rennie, you've got to do it!* Biting harder, she struck another match fast and hard into a flicker of flame! She reached it down to the bracelet and watched but nothing happened until her finger got hot! She dropped it and the other two matches flared up. Rennie jumped back and landed on her bottom.

The flames went out and she stared at the completely whole bracelet. It was black in one area, but when she picked it up, the blackness rubbed onto her fingers.

All the tightness in her body seemed to break and tears came trickling into her eyes. She leaned her chin into her knees.

Now what?

"Renata!" Mama called from the kitchen door. "I told you to weed the garden!"

Rennie jumped up and rubbed her hands across her eyes. "What about Robbie?" she asked quickly, as if that were her excuse. Mama didn't answer and her silence gave Rennie a knot in her stomach.

It also made her mad. Robbie would never weed. He never came home right after school.

But, weeding was the answer! She would bury the bracelet! It wouldn't destroy it, but it would be impossible to find! In the shed, she found a trowel, then tried to deepen the hole which she'd made for the burning. Bits of soil crumbled away under the trowel, but mostly the ground was hard and it pained her hands to dig.

She stood up, planted her hands on her hips, and glanced about the yard. Many times she'd heard people complain about the rockiness of the soil in Whitney Pier and the difficulties of growing a lawn and garden. Their own lawn and garden looked good, because of Papa's love and care. The soil under the grass might be loose, but she couldn't dig there.

That left the garden. She walked up and down the rows surveying the tiny plants, so smooth and green and healthy. They were getting thicker by the day, and the middle of one of those rows would be the perfect place to bury something that you didn't want found, but every leaf reminded her of Papa. She knew she couldn't take a chance on wrecking a single root.

Instead, she dug a hole in a corner of the garden near the lawn where no plants were actually growing. When it was five or six inches deep, she dropped the bracelet in and took a final look at it. No, the bracelet was not nice, not pretty at all. She packed the earth back over it tightly. She brushed the dirt from her hands.

Done! And glad!

She knelt down to weed. The soil was cool and soft under her knees. The tiny plants were tender and sad. She looked them over protectively —*Little orphans in the war, and I'll be their nursemaid.*

She checked the tomato plants that were growing straight and sturdy. Carefully, she rubbed the sucker leaves from between the branches. *You're stealing food from babies. We don't want you.*

After a time, she sat back and looked over the whole garden. There were flower buds on the tomatoes. They were the tallest plants. She would keep them that way. Suddenly, she jumped up and ran into the house.

"Mama! Papa didn't stake the tomatoes! They'll fall over when they get big!"

"He didn't have a chance, *cara.*"

Rennie felt the importance of this. "I'm gonna do it. I saw the stakes in the shed. Papa always does it before the roots get too big so he doesn't hurt them."

Mama caressed her hair. "That's right," she smiled, "and it would be wonderful if you would do that."

This was joy. The following day she carefully tapped a stake down beside each tomato plant. Every little tap was like a prayer to bring Papa home.

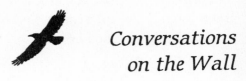

Conversations on the Wall

In two weeks, school was out for the summer. Slowly, Rennie was getting used to being ignored by Julie, and by many of the other non-Italian kids, too. At least they weren't being mean.

Perhaps their parents had warned them about that. Still, not playing with Julie hurt a lot.

The bakery had become a gathering place for grownups. Rick and Serge worked there all day and Mama joined them when the housework was finished. Mama's friends came every afternoon to buy their bread and cakes and sit on chairs that lined the wall where the pictures had been. Rennie kept a game of Parcheesi, some cards, and old movie star paper dolls in the back room where she hung around with Anna and Pietra, hoping for a few scraps of pastry to munch on. Business had fallen off badly and Mama was giving almost nothing away.

"Everyone suffers in times like this!" someone would exclaim.

The talk of the grownups was distressing and Rennie was trying not to hear it. But sometimes the words, along with the anger and despair, seemed to bombard her ears.

Helen Hobinsky went on about all the helpful things Papa had done for community people. "But they see only that he helps Italians, no one else. So, he must love Mussolini! Nonsense!"

Signora Scioppa lamented, "It's all stupid! Now that they've closed the mines, no one eats good!"

Mrs. Bern was thoughtful. "No, but . . . the men wouldn't work with the Italians. Closing them down was the only fair thing to do. That way, everyone suffers the same."

Luisa Da Vita threw her hands up. "Wonderful! And my husband's business is idle. So we all starve together."

"In war, no one wants to understand the other," Mrs. Hobinsky tried to explain.

"So! What do I feed my babies now? *Polenta* and what you English people call porridge. That's all."

Signora Scioppa sighed. "Do you remember," she asked the Italian ladies, "when some of us had hope in Mussolini? He would bring jobs and roads and good government to the old country? And now, look."

"Yes," said Mama, "some thought that. Some would dream of anything for Italy. Most of us over here knew nothing about Mussolini. Now, I have barely enough money for two good meals a day, but I can't make them send Cosimo back."

When Rennie lay her head down at night, her mind woke up and the tiny flowers on her walls became a thousand faces speaking the conversations of the day. Sometimes, horrified, she found that her eyes were wet and she would rub the wetness into her pillow.

She remembered everything about Papa and her together. He took her to school on her very first day, when she was six, because he wanted to. His step was cheerful all the way there and he'd laughed at the nuns, "They think they're so mighty! Wait till they see a father bringing his daughter to school!"

She remembered how he'd coaxed her to make bread. "You push and pull and make your hands strong! You get smooth, sweet dough, that smells so good in the oven!" His face fell in disappointment every time she refused to try it.

She remembered him patiently tightening her roller skates and watching her take off down the sidewalk.

She remembered him hugging her when she was grumpy and telling her she was the most prickly porcupine this side of the Atlantic. She would say, "Then you couldn't hold me so tight." Papa would laugh, *"E vero!"* ("that's true!") and hug her more tightly.

She remembered, also, the time she stayed at Julie's all day while the rest of the family canned tomatoes for winter. She could almost hear his tyrant voice, *"This, signorina, is how you treat your family?"* and the stinging switch he smacked across her backside, making her scream.

She hoped Papa remembered the good things because she missed him so much and she knew how special he was. In the quiet dark of her room, she might let the tears trickle down the sides of her face until her hair was drenched and her sadness ached all the way through her.

How could she help? The garden was Papa's. He'd planted it. Besides, the harvest wouldn't be until fall. What could she do that would help the family *right now?* Something that was only hers and that would make Papa proud?

Finally, one day in July, when Rennie came home from playing with Anna and Pietra, Mama met her at the door, her eyes all flushed with wetness, but a strange and happy smile on her face. She put an arm around Rennie's shoulder and guided her rapidly to the kitchen. "A letter came from Papa!

Sit! Sit! I will read it to you! Oh, Rena! He is all right! He is not home, but he is all right! Listen!"

Rennie sat down and, joyfully, looked into Mama's glowing face. Mama seemed to have words again, thoughts to share, a little happiness, like her old self. That, Rennie found herself thinking, was as good as hearing from Papa. But, oh, to know Papa was safe! She listened raptly as Mama read:

My dear Caterina and children,

What a worry this is for you! I am so sorry! I'm at a camp in Ontario called Petawawa. There are about 500 Italians here. In a way, that is lucky for us, because we can use our own language. That gives us much comfort, and friendships are good. So, though we are prisoners, we are not entirely miserable.

Camp Petawawa is in a beautiful forest but barbed wire fence surrounds us. We have good food and shelter and are taken into the forest everyday to cut wood for our furnaces and stoves. I make all the bread for the men in my section, and that too is a comfort. We can walk around the camp, so do not worry. I am safe and not frightened for myself.

It is terrible not to speak to you and hug you. We can write only three letters of 24 lines every month, and you can do the same. But remember that the soldiers will read your letters before they give them to me.

When will I be home? I do not know! But you, my dear, dear family! How are you? They'll send you a few dollars a month from my work cutting trees, but it will not be much. Riccardo, I hope you are managing the bakery! Sergio, I hope you were not hurt at the mines! Is it true they are closed? My daughters and little son, I hope you are good to your mama and each other! What, what, are you doing for money? These are my 24 lines. Arrivederci, *my dear ones.*

All my love,
Cosimo and Papa

With a happy sad lump in her throat, Rennie watched Mama put down the letter then urgently take Rennie's cheeks in her hands. "It is so good! It is so bad! What shall we do?" Mama cried.

"Write to him, Mama. Can we? I know just what I want to tell him." She had swallowed her lump and was smiling. Papa was safe! He wasn't in a jail cell! And she had decided what to do to make him proud and to help the family!

"Yes. We'll all write to him, when we're together. We'll do it tonight."

And that is what they did. They each had four lines and Rick said they must think very carefully about what to say so they wouldn't waste space.

At the kitchen table, under Rick's and Serge's and Loretta's notes, Rennie wrote:

Papa, I was scared when they took you away, but I've been brave. I've only cried a little and I haven't picked on Roberto. I'm going to learn to make breadsticks and sell them to people and make money. Are you surprised and happy?

Those were her four lines, but something worried her. Holding her pen away from the paper, she looked up at Mama intently. "I don't have room to say I love you and I hope you come home soon."

"That's all right," Mama smiled, "Papa already knows that."

Rick said he'd love to teach her to make breadsticks and he didn't remind her that it was *bread*making. Mama said that it was a wonderful idea, but the garden was more important. She must make certain that it was well watered, well weeded, and free of insects because they would need to can all the vegetables they could get for the winter.

"And," Mama cautioned her, "go only to our friends' homes. I won't have you disturbing others."

Rennie frowned at that. How then was she to make people like them again?

But Mama, seeing the look on Rennie's face, raised her eyebrows in warning.

Bread for the Prisoners

The wedding cake models were still there in the window and the bakery was clean, as always. The smell of cinnamon from the morning's doughnuts was strong, and there was even a hint of almonds starting to bake. But Rennie felt sadness mixed with her excitement when she walked in the next day to start her breadsticks.

"Are you sure you want to do this?" Rick asked. It annoyed her that he had doubts. But still, of all her brothers, he was her favourite, so she told herself he was just showing concern.

"Yes." She looked up at him with a serious smile. It saddened her that he wasn't Papa. He was taller and thinner than Papa and his hair was darker because Papa's was gray. And he didn't look right in Papa's apron or smell right with Papa's bread smells. And, of course, he didn't tease the way Papa teased or hug the way Papa hugged. She wanted to work extra hard to make up for the arrest of her father.

But Rick seemed to be waiting for an explanation, so she said, "We need money."

"Yeah," he said thoughtfully, "but we're doing OK. You're just a kid. You shouldn't worry about that."

"I want to." She didn't tell him how she wanted to make Papa proud of her, or how useless she felt knowing Papa was interned (a word she'd put into her head and not forgotten) and there was nothing she could do about it, or how tired she was of people treating her like a baby, or how he just didn't look right in Papa's apron! She thought, though, that it would be OK having Rick teach her to make bread, since he hadn't been begging her for years to do it, as Papa had been. "Is it hard?" she asked.

"No, it's easy. But, look, Rennie, why do you think people will buy your breadsticks? After all, there's not much money around. And the people who are still our friends buy bread from the bakery."

"Because breadsticks are different from ordinary bread! And they'll be pretty. I'm gonna tie them in ribbons from Mama's sewing box."

"OK," Rick sighed, "let's get started."

He took Rennie to the back kitchen where ovens lined one wall and flour-covered tables filled almost the entire space. Heat from the ovens poured into the room, but a ceiling fan spread it around, and Rennie didn't think she'd get too hot. Rick got her a bowl full of flour, and some yeast and water. Rennie was worried about making bread. She had watched Papa knead the dough lots of times. He would roll up his sleeves and she could see the muscles in his arms ripple, and that's why she'd decided it was men's work. She was certain she couldn't keep doing it for the whole long time that Papa did.

Rick turned on a faucet. "First," he said as he held his fingers under the running water to check the temperature, "you have to start the yeast. You put it in water that's just a few degrees warmer than you are. The water has to be warm or the yeast won't rise, but not too warm or you'll kill it. It's like it's alive."

"I know. Papa told me."

"Then maybe you don't need me."

She grimaced. She supposed she'd better be nice. "I guess I do," she said, and Rick showed her how to test the water temperature by running her wrist under the faucet. When it was correct, she ran two cups of it and sprinkled in the yeast and salt. She pulled up a stool and rested her hands and chin on the countertop while she watched the beads of yeast at the bottom of the cup get slowly bigger and softer looking, until they turned into a bubbly mush and floated to the top of the water. "I think it's ready, Rick," she called, and he started her mixing the flour and water in a bowl until they were well blended together. Then he had her turn them out onto the floured counter top to start kneading.

Gingerly, she started pushing the dough. Then harder. Soon she was rolling it under the cup of her hand, back and forth, toward her and away, slowly, gently, soothingly. She didn't really need muscles to do it! Rick watched her for a moment. "You've got a good touch," he said. But soon she was ready to quit. "When can I stop?" she started asking every few seconds.

"Not yet," he'd say.

I'm Papa making bread for the prisoners.

Finally, the dough was ready to bake. She picked it apart, rolled it into smooth balls and then into snakes as if it were clay. She lined the snakes up on a baking sheet. They were different sizes! She bunched them all together, kneaded a few more times, and did the sticks again. She placed them on the sheet beside each other, perfectly, with a loud sigh for each stick.

I'm so good, they'll send me home.

"You certainly are an impatient little monkey," Rick teased her as he put the dough sticks in the oven. At that, her face grew as hot as the oven, and she determined she'd show no more signs of complaint.

It's good I don't like it. It keeps me brave like Papa. We'll both keep smiling and he'll come home.

For twenty minutes she wandered around the kitchen breathing in the warm bread smell that makes people love bakeries. She peeked into barrels of silky-looking icing sugar and smooth, oval almonds, tempted to touch, but knowing she shouldn't. There were bins of plump raisins and a refrigerator filled with milk and butter and fresh strawberries and rhubarb that would be turned into pies before the day was out. There was a chocolate pie, too, like the last one Papa sold to Julie.

But I won't think of that. I'll be happy like Papa when he's in the bakery.

She had a collection of ribbons from home. When the breadsticks were baked and cooled, she gathered them in fours, crusty brown and smooth, and tied them with bows. She had three bunches with pink ribbons, four with blue, two yellows, a green and two purple. A rainbow's dozen. She'd thought she'd have a lot more than that, but for the first day that was OK. They were beautiful. They'd sell quickly and tomorrow she could make twice as many.

"Wonderful!" Rick exclaimed. The sun seemed to shine from Rennie's face. She loaded the breadsticks gently into a paper bag and headed out into the neighborhood.

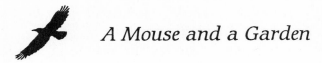 *A Mouse and a Garden*

It was a sunny day in Whitney Pier. The sky was blue and the factory wasn't belching its red dust as Rennie began her trek. Her breadsticks pleased her and people on the streets looked cheerful.

Nevertheless, she went to Mrs. Hobinsky's first, for good luck. It was an easy sale and Mrs. Hobinsky gave her an extra nickle for extra good luck, but she warned Rennie, "Don't you get too disappointed if they don't all go. With the mine closed down, people are poor, you know."

"They only cost a nickle, Mrs. Hobinsky."

"That doesn't matter, dear. And another thing," she said after a moment's pause, "if anyone says anything that's a little hurtful, don't you pay them any mind. You're a good, thoughtful girl, and that's what counts."

"I won't," Rennie frowned. It hadn't occurred to her that that might happen, despite all the terrible words of the past few weeks. After all, she was offering people something lovely and tasty.

She walked down Mrs. Hobinsky's path. The old horsechestnut in her yard was probably the biggest tree in all of Whitney Pier. Rennie left the path so she could stand right under it and look up. It umbrella'd high above her head, blocking out the blue with dark, delicious green. The leaves were thick and well fed.

She skipped up the path through the next yard. It, too, looked healthy. The door was a forest green. Through its small square window peeked an older woman she recognized from visits to the bakery. "Yes?" the woman asked curiously when she opened the door. Rennie suddenly discovered how shy she felt. She almost never spoke to adults, unless she knew them really well.

"Would you like to buy some breadsticks, M'am?" She held out a golden bunch in a pink ribbon.

"Why, that would be lovely!" Soon she was dropping a nickle, kerplunk, into the bottom of Rennie's bag.

"Thank you!" Rennie smiled as she skipped back down the path.

Only go to friends, she remembered.

But at the next house, a fluffly white terrier wagged its tail at her. She bent down and petted him all over as he wiggled in joy. *Everyone* in Whitney Pier was a friend. She gave the dog a big hug and ran up to the door. Here, some teenagers joked with each other, "I think I'm a little hungry, are you?" "Oh, for sure, I haven't eaten in days!" They each bought a bunch and the sun kept shining.

There were a few refusals — but the Scioppas and the Da Vita's bought from her. People were friendly and she was feeling fine.

Soon she was on Julie's block. She could still feel a smile on her face. They hadn't spoken in a month — but Julie liked pretty things: blue skies, colourful ribbons, shiny bread.

She hurried down the street and turned into Julie's walk. Something moved from behind the house. Mr. McLean was cutting the grass in the backyard. His t-shirt clung to him in patches of sweat and he pushed the lawnmower, clackety clack, like the teeth of giants. The coal miners were still out of work and still hating the Italians because of it.

Quickly, before he saw her, she ran to the front door. She'd stood right here a thousand times before! She rang the bell.

Julie answered.

"Hi, Julie!"

"What do you want?" Julie demanded.

Then Rennie knew the stupid thing she'd done.

But she was trapped. Like a mouse. "Would your mom like to buy some breadsticks?"

"Don't be stupid."

"Julia!" Mrs. McLean snapped from behind her. "Don't speak to her." Mrs. McLean shoved herself in front of Julie. Her eyes pierced like a witch's. "You should know better than to be here," she said to Rennie. She shut the door hard. Rennie stood there. It was as if her brain had stopped and her feet were glued down. The door was black, but she stared at it as if she could see through it, or as if it hadn't shut. Then suddenly everything changed. Why had she gone there? Had she forgotten this was war? *Revenge?*

She turned and walked defiantly away. She would not be sad! She would sell the rest of her breadsticks bravely and show Julie!

Or, show herself.

She stomped along. When would the anger fade?

"Good morning, Rennie!" Who was that? A woman she'd just stomped past.

She turned. It was Mrs. Bern, one of the nicest ladies in town.

"Good morning, Mrs. Bern."

Mrs. Bern caught up to her so they were walking along together. "Are you having a nice day?"

Rennie was slowly feeling friendly again. Mrs. Bern was lovely. She had sparkling green eyes like a cat and soft reddish hair that fell in wispy strands around her cheek, making her look almost childlike. She liked children, too. She always spoke to them.

"I guess so," said Rennie. "I'm selling breadsticks."

"Are you? Well, I'd like some of those. Here we are at my house. Come on in while I find some money."

She sat Rennie down at the kitchen table and gave her juice, crackers and grape jelly. She sat with her and started talking as if they were continuing a conversation.

"You must not worry. When this war is over, the world will be a much better place. Hitler and Mussolini, and men like them, will never again be loose. Your daddy will be safe. So will everyone, everywhere. You mustn't worry." She sat at the table and nodded her head sympathetically in Rennie's direction. "It is hard for you. What they've done to your daddy is a terrible thing. But they will see their mistake. This war — it is a good thing," she assured Rennie.

Rennie could hardly believe it. "Why?" she whispered. *They took my papa!* Without thinking, she crunched a cracker between her fingers. A crumby mess coated her hand and fell on the table in front of her. She didn't dare look at Mrs. Bern or brush off her hand. She held it on the table, closed and still.

Gently, Mrs. Bern put her own hand on top of Rennie's and they looked at each other. Her eyes smiled.

"Because Hitler wants to take over the world. He is killing thousands of people just because he doesn't like them. Jewish people, like Dr. Bern and me. We have to stop him from doing these terrible things."

Rennie was looking hard at Mrs. Bern. How could anyone not like her? "Why?" she asked again.

"Why what, dear?"

"Why doesn't Hitler like you?"

"Because Jews have a different religion than him. He thinks there should only be Protestants. Some people say he wants only tall, blond people in the world and most Jewish people are different than that. And many work hard and have very good jobs. Hitler thinks the Jews will take over the world."

Rennie was silent. She had wanted comfort, but now, on top of her anger, she was scared. She tried to act normal while she spread some jelly on a cracker, but her hand shook again and the cracker broke up. Purple jelly smeared into the table cloth. How was she going to keep from crying?

Mrs. Bern gently took the knife and fixed a cracker for her. "What is it, Rennie?"

"My papa is Catholic! And he works hard!" Rennie blurted out.

"Yes. And maybe people in our country are acting a little like Hitler. But they will see their mistake and when this war is over, your daddy will be home."

Rennie was breathing hard. Everything was terrible —the whole world! But when she looked up again, she saw that Mrs. Bern was almost laughing. She toussled Rennie's hair and said, "Here I've been talking on and on! And I thought it was your people who were the talkative types!"

"What do you mean?"

Mrs. Bern laughed again. "Never mind! Here! Two nickles! I'm hungry this afternoon. Now you go sell the rest of those and have a good time doing it."

Rennie got up and walked slowly to the door. "Mrs. Bern," she asked, "when will the war be over?"

Mrs. Bern put her hand on Rennie's shoulder. "Well, now, no one knows the answer to that. It will take as long as it takes for the right side to win. That's the side that will set your daddy free."

As Rennie walked around the neighbourhood, Mrs. Bern's words burned in her mind. Fear tightened her stomach. Each face was a goblin and she was its food — perfect food.

She didn't smile once after that and there were many no thank you's. There was a "Certainly not!" that made her jump. But she wasn't arrested or beaten or killed. She was only Rennie Trani. She wasn't anyone who could take over the world. She had two bunches of breadsticks left when she reached her street again, but she felt she couldn't knock on another door. Julie had jinxed her day.

Maxie, the policeman's daughter, came flying down the sidewalk on her roller skates. *We are at war with Italy, her father said. Come with us.*

Rennie planted her feet right in front of Maxie. Maxie grabbed her arms to keep from falling, but Rennie landed on her bottom with Maxie on top of her. The pain went through her thin shorts like a spanking for both of them.

"Hey, why'd you do that?"

"Leave me alone!" Rennie pushed herself to her feet. "I hate you!"

Maxie looked up at her with her mouth hanging open. Suddenly Rennie felt sorry. It wasn't Maxie who deserved punishing. "What did I do?" asked Maxie.

Rennie just shuffled her feet.

"Well," Maxie stood up and looked at Rennie questioningly, "what do you have in the bag?"

Rennie answered slowly, "Breadsticks. They're a nickle for four."

"Oh! Yummy! I'll go get Daddy. He's home right now."

"No!" said Rennie, but Maxie gave her a confused look and ran into the house anyway. She came back with Sgt. MacPhee. He was shaking some coins in his hand and smiling pleasantly.

"What have you got there?" he asked. When he saw what she was selling, he bought Rennie's two remaining bunches. "Won't you come in and enjoy them with us?"

But you arrested my father! "I — I — can't. It's time for supper."

"Another time, then," offered Sgt. MacPhee, "and keep up the good work."

She gave him a confused smile. "OK," she said.

She went home and walked around to the soothing greenness of her garden. She was shaking inside and there was a ball of tears in her throat ready to burst. She clutched the rolled up paper bag of nickles tightly. She looked over the row of tomatoes. They had grown half as high as the stakes and were covered with tiny green fruits where flowers had been. The leaves were fuzzy and soft. Her fingers relaxed and she touched one.

She laid her bag on the grass. She crouched down to adjust a soft strip of cloth which she'd used to tie a vine to a stake. Very gently, she smoothed it out so that it wasn't cutting into the stalk. She rubbed out the suckers and checked for caterpillars. Her fingers worked as she'd seen Papa's do for years and years.

The tomatoes were such beautiful, delicate plants. Each day from now on she would check them, fixing the cloth strips as the stems got thicker and taller.

She stayed crouched down for a moment, breathing the freshness of the garden. Then she went to the kitchen where Mama was breaking beans and dropping them in a pot. She walked over to the blue spotted pig and frowned at the stupid grin it gave her. She dropped in a nickle. Clink. Snap went a bean. Clink. Snap.

"Well, how'd it go?" asked Mama when the clinking stopped.

Rennie turned toward her. "Good," she said hopefully. Mama looked as if she might be in a good mood. Her hands were lively with the beans and she wore a fresh flowered dress that made her look round and comfortable. It might be nice to hug her and listen to her heartbeat and feel her hotness right through her clothes.

But Mama just said, "I'm glad."

Rennie started towards her room, but something stopped her. She turned around.

"Mama — Sgt. MacPhee bought two bunches."

Mama was very slow to answer, but finally she said, "Yes. He's a good man."

Sgt. MacPhee was good. So how could he have arrested her father? Some day she would figure it out.

In her room, she knelt down by her bed, and prayed for Papa to come home soon. "Please make things better," she whispered in her prayer, "and tell Papa how nice the garden is."

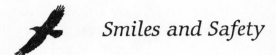 *Smiles and Safety*

After her prayer, Rennie sat on her bed with her legs hanging over the side and her eyes staring at the pink and purple flowers on the wall. What could she do? There was an untidy stack of comic books on a table and some jacks and paper dolls scattered around the floor. How come Mama hadn't told her to clean them up? She should do it just the same, but she had too many bad things to think about. Anyway, soon she'd have to set the table for supper.

She got down on the floor and fiddled with paper dolls. *You're stupid* they said to each other. *You're stupid, I hate you.* Before she knew it, she found the dolls slapping against each other. One of them was Julie and one was her, fighting, fighting.

"Come eat!" Mama's call from the kitchen shook her out of her play. She ran downstairs. The table was already set! And Loretta was just washing her hands.

"Didn't you help cook?" Rennie asked in surprise.

"No. Didn't you?"

Rennie didn't answer that. She just wondered why Mama was doing the work by herself. Again, she felt lonely. She missed the time she spent with Mama, even if often it was in setting the table. And she didn't like Mama being different than before.

The family barely spoke as they sat at the table. Mama asked Serge to say grace, which he did, then he bent his head over his beans and sausage. It made Rennie squirm. Serge had not even noticed the shamrock tablecloth Mama had used.

"Hey, Serge," Rennie said, "look at the tablecloth."

"So?"

"It's the shamrock one."

"So?"

"Well, you hate it 'cause it's for the Irish and not the Italians. You always say Mama shouldn't use it."

"We have other troubles, Rennie." He aimed a sorrowful look toward the end of the table where Papa should be. "Ma," he said, "Papa loves Italy. But didn't he know about Mussolini?"

"What does Mussolini have to do with Italy?"

"He's the leader!" Loretta perked up.

"One man does not make a country."

Loretta wasn't convinced. "Anyway, we're really Canadian."

"We're really both," said Serge. "Sadly for Papa."

Rennie frowned. What language did her family speak? Why was Papa arrested? And who were the people she loved so much? Wasn't it obvious? She had to say it, "Only Italian things are good."

As she said it, the smiling eyes of Mrs. Bern appeared to her, but Mama cut in. "That's a foolish way to talk, *signorina*." She gave Rennie a hard, steady look that forced her to lower her eyes. Rennie had meant it when she first said it, but — was she being a little like Hitler?

There was silence after that. Rick looked thoughtful, with his hand around a glass of Papa's red wine, and he caught Rennie's eye and smiled. But the wine reminded her of Mr.

McLean and Papa's arrest and Hitler —frightening thoughts that filled the quiet. Would no one talk?

"I'm tired of the same old food every night!" That would get Mama talking. "How come we can't have lasagna or osso buco? That's my favorite." Osso buco was a delicious veal stew made with spices and wine, and Rennie knew it cost too much.

"You know why," said Mama.

"Well, this is boring!"

"*Are you looking for a fight?*" At that, Rennie knew she'd better be quiet. She looked at her plate and felt her nose squinch up. She was only trying to liven things up. Mrs. Hobinsky, Mrs. Bern and Sgt. MacPhee were all lively people and all talked even if she didn't. And they made her feel good.

"Were people friendly today?" Rick asked her.

"Not everybody." She was glad that he spoke. "But I wasn't very friendly, either. Tomorrow I'm gonna smile a whole lot and talk a lot. And I'm gonna make twice as many breadsticks."

Rick rubbed the back of his head and narrowed his eyes for a minute. Then he said, "I think that will be too much work. Besides, you didn't do anything wrong. It's just not a good time for people."

She felt her prickles stand up! "Don't tell me what to do!"

"*Renata, upstairs,*" ordered Mama.

Robbie grinned and Rennie gave him a nasty look. She carried her half-eaten sausage and beans to the counter and went to her room.

Well, she had been unfriendly, after all. And to her own family! She stood in front of the mirror wondering how she could spread enough friendliness to stop the war. "Do you want any breadsticks?" she said to the mirror. No, said the mirror. She tried again, smiling, tilting her head a little, sounding so polite, "I have some delicious, fresh breadsticks that I made myself. Would you be interested in buying some?" She tried to be the people with their doors wide open. "Yes, I would! How nice! What a lovely idea! I'll buy them all!" She changed her smiles. Wide ones. Little ones. Teeth showing, teeth covered. Eyes large, eyes slanted. *I'll buy them all, I'll buy them all, I'll buy them* . . . Her smiles turned to frowns. Nothing seemed quite right. She lay down on her bed. With her eyes half closed, she saw the big strong doors swing toward her.

It was as if she knew that the selling would get worse, and it did. Each day, fewer people bought her breadsticks until, one day, she straggled into her back yard and dropped her bag on the ground without caring about it. In it were 10 nickles and 14 bundles of breadsticks. Every "no thank you" had sounded like a storm.

She looked over the garden from a distance. It was a comforting green from one end to the other with soft leaves at different heights, cheery flowers here and there, and a light, sweet fragrance that hovered over everything. Papa could be proud of *that*.

Her frown turned upwards without her knowing and she went to start weeding. She crawled up and down the rows, pulling out seedlings as tiny as her pinky fingernail, until finally her legs ached and she sat back to rest. There in front of her, was a taller weed. How had she missed it? She reached to yank it out, but then she stopped herself. She eased it out carefully by the roots. She pulled off leaves one by one. *It's an explosive like in the war. I have to take it apart piece by piece so it won't hurt anyone. And I have to be very careful or it will blow me apart!*

She knelt by a tomato plant and felt the refreshing earth under the palm of her hand. She packed it against the roots of the plant. *Goodnight little child in the war. I can keep you safe from the soldiers and bombs.*

She sprayed fine mists of water everywhere. It was rain in the forests where Papa chopped wood each day, drenching him. No, *I'm clouds raining on the gardens at Petawawa so Papa will have good healthy food.* . . . Were there gardens at Petawawa?

She watered the spot where the bracelet was buried, making it sink deeper and deeper into the soil where it would never be found. . . . Could she *really* make it sink?

Robbie came zipping across the grass on his bicycle. "Why are you watering *there?*" He let the bike fall heavily as he jumped to the ground.

She was startled out of her dreams, nearly yelling, *because Julie deserves it!* Luckily, she didn't. "I'm just finishing! Where have you been? You haven't helped in a week!"

"So?"

She almost continued the argument, but then she remembered she was going to be nice, for Papa, for Mama, for the whole angry world.

Anyway, who needed Robbie? The garden was looking good by her own efforts, even if the bread selling was going badly.

Suddenly, she had an idea.

"Please finish watering the beans, Robbie. I've got to do something." She handed him the hose and went to the shed for stakes and a roll of burlap. Papa had everything he needed for gardening placed around in an orderly fashion. She took some scissors, cut off a wide piece of burlap and found string.

Out in the garden, Robbie was poking his fingers in the spray of water that came from the hose. It splashed everywhere except on the beans. Rennie bit her tongue and walked to the tomato vine at the far end of the row. With the end of the scissors, she banged three stakes into the soil to make a square corner around the north side of the plant. She thought the north winds were coldest.

"What are you doing?" Robbie knotted his face together.

"Making a windbreak."

"A what?"

"It protects the plant from the winds." He was looking and sounding just like a toad, but Rennie put her mind on her work.

How could she tie the floppy cloth to the stakes so it didn't drag to the ground and so it ended up straight, like a flat curtain going around a corner? She gathered it up — it was long and scratchy with see-through holes between all the threads. It had a weird straw smell. She liked it.

She stretched most of it over two stakes and poked a string through some of its holes at an end. This she tied around the top of the first stake. She tied the middle and other end to the remaining stakes in the same manner. Robbie gave her a strange look, then dropped the hose so the spray shot towards the sky. "Dumb!" he yelled, grabbing his bike and riding off.

Rennie stood back to check her work. A little wrinkled, but not bad. She flattened it all over, making it hang as evenly as possible. Then she poked more string through holes and tied it tightly to each stake in six places.

She looked the whole thing over with her lips together and her hands on her hip. She had a good strong screen she'd made herself. It felt and looked like the earth and made a cozy corner for her tomato plant. She rubbed one of the plant's leaves between her fingers. *You're my special tomato vine. I'll make you grow the biggest tomatoes Papa ever saw. By the time they're ripe, he'll be home!*

Swinging Chains and Slamming Doors

Rennie sprang to a sitting position. Blackness enclosed her and she clutched her blanket. Demons were tearing wildly through the garden. Red eyed and gruesome, they smashed around, swinging silvery chains and ripping at the plants. Help us! Help us! the plants cried, but a black door slammed and then there was nothing. Certainly not! said a sharp voice.

She drew up her knees and bit into her blanket. Ouch! She'd bitten her finger. She looked around. It was only her bedroom that was dark and Loretta was breathing deeply in the bed beside her, but she felt sweaty.

Though she could still see the images of the nightmare, her breath began to come more easily. She could smell a strong salt breeze from the sea and there was a high whistling as the wind screeched through the corners of the house. A small twig with leaves battered the window and flew off again. There *was* a storm outside. The tomatoes!

She ran downstairs in her nightgown, forgetting shoes and robe. The back door nearly flew off the hinges when she opened it. The plants in the garden were whipping about wildly, but there was no rain, only violent wind. One of the bean trellises had fallen, but she fought her way to her favourite tomato vine. It was standing. The windbreak she'd built so well was taking most of the wind, but it thrashed about uncertainly. How long would it last? She stood behind it and spread out her nightgown trying to break the wind herself.

You can't get through. I'll keep you away forever. My tomatoes will be the best in the world.

A weed that grew over the bracelet grave was being blown to the ground over and over again. Rennie had a feeling that the bracelet had come undug. She searched the ground with her eyes. The wind whipped at her shoulders, but she saw nothing except darkness and bare feet frozen to the soil. Where was the bracelet? She felt certain it was lying behind a plant. She had to find it before someone else did, but she couldn't leave the tomato vine. Tears streamed down her cheeks. Her hair beat up and down, stinging the sides of her face as it fell.

"Rennie! For heaven's sakes!" Rick came running towards her. He took off his robe and wrapped it around her, then picked her up and carried her to the house. She buried her face in his shoulder and cried until she could cry no more.

They were sitting in the kitchen by then. Slowly, the warmth from Rick's arms seeped into her. Pictures from the nightmare drifted in and out behind her closed eyelids and the memory of the wind on her shoulders made her shudder. As if nothing worse could happen, she whispered, "My tomato vine is going to die."

"Your windbreak is strong, Rennie. It's good protection."

She believed him because she couldn't stand not to. Nor could she stand to have anyone know how frightened she was.

"Please don't tell Mama about tonight."

"Our secret," he promised.

After a few hours' sleep in her own bed, she woke up and pulled on shorts and a blouse. Still barefoot, she went outside in the cool, wet grass of the morning. What would she find? She walked around the garden to the far side where the tomato vine was.

To her amazement, it looked beautiful. In fact, most of the garden had survived the windstorm well. It gave her courage to keep up with the breadsticks.

Later that day, as she pushed and pulled the soft, smooth dough, nightmare thoughts mixed with everyday thoughts like in a painting. There were the demons again, but this time they were throwing around the bracelet, not a chain! The garden was being destroyed. She had saved it, and lucky, too, because everyone else was slamming doors. Just like when she tried to sell breadsticks, only those doors didn't really slam — she knew that.

They just closed firmly, sometimes in the middle of sentences, or with just a shake of a head. Sometimes a curtain at a window was pulled back and then the door never opened at all.

On a gray Monday, a wet fog floated around Rennie. It misted her nose with a soft coolness. For a moment she smiled, but then she saw little drops of water on her crisp brown crusts. The bread would turn soggy. She wiped at the droplets with her hand but the water just spread out. She could hide the bread under the big white sweater but she wasn't wearing it. Suddenly her arms got cold.

She'd have to finish her selling quickly. She pressed the bag of bread close to her chest and began walking fast. All the people at this end of the block had stopped buying from her a long time ago, so she kept going. The drops of mist were getting a little bigger. It was turning to rain. She leaned forward so the rain would fall on the back of her shoulders instead of the bread, but it didn't help.

At the end of the street were some mothers she barely knew. Their children were much younger than Rennie and they went to the Protestant church. Still, sometimes they bought from her.

They were urging little kids on tricycles to move along. If she could only keep the bread safe until she got to them.

She unbuttoned the front of her blouse and shoved the bag next to her skin. She kept moving fast. The sharp paper bag edges and breadcrusts prickled.

"Excuse me," she said, catching her breath as she caught up to the people. They had opened umbrellas and were walking in two tight groups to keep out of the rain. Rennie put on a smile and pushed her discomfort away. "Would you like some bread today? Maybe the kids are hungry."

"Yes!" said some of the little ones. "Rennie's breadsticks! We want some!"

"But where are they?" One of the mothers was eyeing Rennie's blouse.

"Oh, here," Rennie pulled them out. "I had to keep them dry."

"Under your shirt!" The woman threw her hand to her chest as if stricken. Rennie's mouth dropped open. She took a step back and swallowed hard.

The other mother narrowed her eyes and pushed her face towards Rennie. Her voice was low and hard. "We can't eat them when they've been next to your skin. Haven't you got more sense than that?"

Witches. Screeching. Scratching.

Rennie stepped back again, then turned to run, but there was a tricycle right there. She tripped over it, banging a hip on the handlebar and landing with a knee and both hands on the sidewalk. Her breadsticks were lying on the ground, cracked, and the nickles spread away from her in a nearly straight line. The pavement was gray with wetness. The child on the trike screamed. Though she wanted to crumple up right there, she pulled herself up and ran, leaving everything.

How could she have been so stupid? How could she have left her nickles! Could she run fast enough to reach the garden before she cried?

But she met Mama on the sidewalk going to the bakery. They stopped. Rennie bit her trembling lip while Mama looked her over. Then Rennie burst into tears.

Inside, Mama got a soft cloth and washed her wounds with warm, soapy water. Then they sat close together on the sofa. How could Rennie tell why she felt so badly?

But Mama wasn't rushing her. She seemed to be thinking hard. Finally she said, "That's the end of your selling."

Rennie pulled away from her and cried, "Why?"

"Because you've gone to many people you shouldn't have gone to. And look how unhappy you are."

"But I have to! You can't make me stop! I *won't* stop!"

"What you will do, miss, is stop shouting and obey me."

Rennie ran outside and stomped her feet on the back steps. She pounded her fist on the railing and then, to calm herself, she folded her arms tightly across her chest. The rain pattered at her skin in cold drops. She walked slowly to the tomato rows. She peered at them intently until her eyes fell on a huge green tomato caterpillar. She pulled it off and crushed it into the mud with her heel. "Haven't you got more sense than to eat my tomatoes?" she hollered.

She turned around to find Mama standing there watching her anger. She hung her head.

She could feel the squeak in her own voice." I need to earn money, and I need Papa to be proud of me."

"Papa is *very* proud of you. A letter came from him. Wait till you read it. And listen! I've saved all your nickles. Let's use them to buy sugar and almonds and make Papa some *amaretti*. We'll send him a package tied with ribbons. He'll love that!"

"Can we?" Rennie brightened.

"Yes. Now come in out of the rain." Inside, Mama pointed to the part in the letter that Rennie should read. It was four lines just for her.

Renata, now you are like me! You see how good the silky dough makes you feel? It was a lucky thing they brought me to Petawawa so you could learn about bread. I am so proud of all your help, my little porcupine!

Rennie's face glowed. "Does kneading the dough make you feel good?" Mama asked.

Rennie thought about it. "At first it does. But I get tired of it really fast."

"Then it is time to play again."

Rennie nodded, then, seeing Mama's warm face, she hugged her. She was feeling relieved and sad all at once. She had the garden which was plenty of work, and that was very special to Papa. But giving up breadmaking meant completely giving up her efforts with the neighbours.

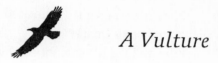 *A Vulture*

Robbie came charging across the grass on his bike. Right at the edge of the garden he did a wild wheelie and then jumped off, letting the bike spin to the ground with a thud.

Rennie screamed, "The cauliflower!" The bike had landed across two cauliflower plants that had just come ripe, breaking the fruits into pieces. One of them was to be dinner that night. She couldn't believe how awful she felt. In two and a half months, she'd grown to love the garden almost as if it were Papa.

Robbie saw the look on her face and said, in a small voice, "Gosh, I didn't mean it." She turned away from him, keeping her angry words to herself.

In a moment his voice got brighter. "Rennie, I was in a rush to tell you something. That's why it happened. Don't you want to hear?"

"No." Without meaning to, she walked to the bracelet grave and stood over it protectively. For some reason, the thought of Julie had entered her mind. Robbie gave her a curious look, but he didn't say anything and she sighed a small relief. She had let the weed grow over the grave to make it look uncared for and Robbie had no reason to suspect anything. To keep him from thinking too long, she asked, "OK. What?"

"I met Julie and she has a message for you. When school starts, don't talk to her, don't look at her, don't come near any of her friends on the playground. If you do, she'll say a prayer that Papa never comes home."

"I don't believe it!" shouted Rennie. "You're lying!"

"Cross my heart!"

"I'm telling Mama about the cauliflower! She'll make you eat it raw, piece by piece, right off the ground! I'm telling her you lied and she'll write to Papa! You'll be sorry you ever made up such a hateful, hateful thing!" She ran to the kitchen and did just as she said.

But Mama, who was cooking with Loretta, answered her shortly, "It's silly to worry about Julie after all this time. And bring in the cauliflower. It's still edible."

Rennie grabbed a bowl and stormed outside. She ordered Robbie to move his bike, then klunked the broken bits of vegetable into the bowl. How unfair it was! How stupid she felt! How mean people were!

But, what did Robbie and Mama have to do with it? Rennie rushed the bowl into the kitchen, dropped it on the table and was out the front door fast.

She'd tell Julie a thing or two! She'd show her who could be mean!

It was a hot night. The McLeans were in their backyard getting ready to eat, it seemed. Rennie had a sudden stab of fear. She didn't want to see Julie's parents. She stopped a little way down the street to watch them.

Mrs. McLean was putting food on the picnic table and Mr. McLean and Julie were running around laughing. Julie had the hose and was spraying her father. He was spreading his arms out and wiggling his tongue at her and looking really dumb.

Or fun. He had that same grin he wore the day he took Julie and Rennie rafting on the peaceful Mira River. They kept pushing him over into the water. He kept coming up and spraying water through a snorkel at them. Then he tipped the raft over and grabbed them each under the chin and back kicked all the way to shore. The three of them kept laughing. Mr. McLean was strong and warm and jolly.

Rennie no longer felt like shouting and pushing.

But her hatred kept growing.

She walked to the fence and stood staring at all of them. When Julie noticed her, Rennie called out, "You'll be sorry, Julie McLean. Your brother will get killed and it will be all your fault. Bad things happen to bad people."

She waited for them to do something. When would they holler at her? When would Julie throw a tomato? Something had frozen a look of horror on their faces.

Mr. McLean moved first. His huge body came barrelling forward. He pointed his finger, "See here . . . !" Rennie ran, but she heard him shouting after her, "What you need is to be turned over your father's knee!"

What had he said? She slowed down — but she kept on going until she rounded the corner out of sight. Then she stopped and crouched down, hugging her knees to her chest. *Papa would never let me be so mean.*

When she was finally able to get up, she walked on home like a snail.

She picked at her supper. Who cared about Mr. McLean? It was her terrible words that mattered, your brother will be killed, killed. Shouldn't she be happy? She'd done what she wanted.

Mama, who'd been watching her, said, "I'm not angry with you, Renata. I snapped at you because I was upset."

Rennie had forgotten about that, but Mama went on, "Your brothers might have to join the army."

Rennie's forehead furrowed into a deep frown and the smell of her fried potatoes was suddenly sickening. She looked quickly to Rick who was trying to smile while he chewed.

He finally swallowed his mouthful and assured his mother there was nothing to worry about. "They won't be calling men as young as us unless the war gets much worse."

"Which it will," said Mama.

Now Rennie swallowed hard. She thought again of the McLeans staring at her, frozen. She thought of her brothers being killed. For the first time, the war seemed real.

She searched her brain for something hopeful. "Mrs. Bern said it's a good war," she offered.

"A good war that takes your papa prisoner and then asks his sons to fight?"

"She said when the right side wins, Papa will be free."

"There is no right side!" insisted Mama.

Then, does that mean Papa will never be free?

Papa. Rick and Serge. Tom McLean. The Italians. The Jews. How could she have been so mean?

Be good, thought Rennie desperately. Try to be completely good. If *everyone* does that, *then* the war will end.

But lots of other people weren't willing to be good. Late on the following Saturday afternoon, Rennie said good-bye to her friends and dashed to the bakery. It was Rick's last day there. The next morning he was going back to university on his scholarship because there wasn't enough work for all of them in the bakery and Mama thought he was better off doing something useful. Rennie wanted to spend that last half hour watching him shine up the counters, close out the cash register, fold up Papa's apron and drop it in Mama's laundry bag. Rick enjoyed the bakery almost as much as Papa did.

Even though Rick would be leaving, Rennie had a good feeling when she arrived. She smiled at the sound of Serge humming loudly as he wiped down the ovens in the kitchen. The smell of baked blueberries made her pleasantly hungry. Mama tied up a pie for Mrs. Hobinsky. Other customers were buying the last loaves of bread for a few pennies. Mrs. Bern bought some, but she insisted on paying full price. "This bread is just as good as it was first thing in the morning!" she exclaimed. "Not your fault I didn't manage to get here until 4:30!" She flashed her green eyes at Rennie as she left.

"Grazie!" called Mama after her. "That's a good woman," she said to the others.

Signor and Signora Scioppa were there spending pennies, for which Signora apologized.

"We are all in this together," Mama said. The miners were back at work, all except the Italians whom the bosses had finally fired. The Scioppas, as well as the Da Vitas, were living largely on the kindness of neighbours. The five young people at Rennie's house usually left the supper table slightly hungry, but once or twice a week, Mama took sauce and pasta to their friends anyway.

Rennie leaned her elbows on the glass countertop and gazed lovingly into Rick's face. He gave her a teasing grin and put the Scioppas' bread in a paper bag. With a contented smile, he folded the top down into a neat handle for them.

Mama took out the broom to ready the floor for mopping. It looked sparkling, anyway, and Rennie knew she swept about every half hour. But she looked fine with a broom in her hand. Peaceful. For a moment, Rennie felt perfect. She had a perfect family.

Then the door flew open. Immediately, a charge of salt air from the harbour drowned the sweet bakery smells. Three men ploughed in, miners, all of them. Their eyes were red and, for a few moments, they bumbled about clumsily, tripping over their feet, stumbling against the counters. One of them staggered uncomfortably close to Rennie and she backed away at the smell of the tavern on his breath.

Mr. McLean was the leader. He came like a vulture, shiny headed and red nosed. He looked threateningly, first into Mama's eyes, then into Rick's, then, with a hatred that seemed to burn, into Rennie's.

She hurried to Mama's side. Mama held on to the broom like a crutch and squeezed Rennie close to her. Signor and Signora Scioppa backed against a window. Helen Hobinsky stood solid right in the middle of the floor. One of the men spread his arms wide against the door. "No one's leaving," he said.

Mr. McLean slurred a demand. "We want some pies! Where are your pies?"

"There aren't any left," Rick said, staying as calm as possible.

"Three pies and fast!"

"Believe me," but Rick didn't have a chance to finish. The men headed toward the kitchen, only to be met by Serge, a solid scowl across his face, standing at the door.

"I've called the police," he announced forcefully, "You'd better leave."

"Called the police, eh?" Mr. McLean laughed. "A lot good that'll do y'!" He tried pushing his way past Serge, but Serge kept blocking the door until the two of them were shoving at each other.

"You drunken fool," cried Mrs. Hobinsky in disgust, "take this and leave good people alone!" She held out her pie, but he laughed again.

"Get out," warned Serge, "get out before you're sorry."

The other miners were holding back, but Mr. McLean was frightening. He started talking. "Traitors! Living the good life while your countrymen slaughter people overseas! You owe us! Six good weeks of mining lost because of Italian traitors! No pies? We'll see!" He pushed at Serge. Serge pushed back.

Mama was shaking like a leaf and so was Rennie. She had inside her the cold memory of things she had done to Julie. She, an Italian.

Mr. McLean was big, but Serge had a temper. They shoved until, finally, Serge shouldered him in a football tackle and pushed him backwards. His feet scrambled under him and his face went beastly, but he recovered. He stood catching his breath, getting ready to charge.

They are two explosives, ready to blow! You can take them apart!

Though she had a terrible fear in the pit of her stomach, Rennie burst free from Mama and ran to Mr. McLean. Frantically she looked up into his pale blue eyes. They were rimmed in red like one of her demons. But she knew that he could smile.

"Mr. McLean! Please stop! Julie's my friend!"

He stopped panting and focussed those eyes on her. His body seemed to sink a bit as he gazed at her. "Your friend?" he repeated in amazement. He wiped at his brow, turned slowly, and walked out the door.

The other men shuffled out behind him. Mama came and drew Rennie into her arms. She buried her face in Rennie's hair and whispered, *"Grazie Dio."*

Rennie held her, too, but not in quite the little girl way she had before. She felt bigger.

No Witch Can Hurt Me

School started. Rennie and Julie were in the same class, and that was the worst thing ever. Rennie had such a terrible mix of angry and sorrowful feelings for Julie, and she also missed her a lot. They couldn't talk at all, though, because Julie hated her.

But, Julie was surrounded by hate.

Now that Rennie knew better, she *had* to fix things.

She had to find a quiet spot to talk. She would just die if she tried to be nice and Julie was mean and someone else heard. For a few days she watched Julie on the playground, waiting for her to be alone somewhere — in a corner, or by the gate coming in, or after her friends had all run to the line up. It never happened. How could it be that a person *always* had people near her?

Finally, she couldn't wait another day. She hung around the edges of Julie's crowd at recess, staying far enough away that they ignored her. At the first moment that Julie stepped a little to the side, Rennie moved between her and her friends, trying to look calm.

"Julie," she said, butterflies flitting around her stomach, "how's Tom?"

In surprise, Julie shot out, "What's it to you?"

"Just leave me alone." Julie walked away, but in that short time, the crowd of kids had moved near.

"Yeah, leave her alone," someone said to Rennie. "Yeah," said someone else. "Italian traitor."

Rennie tried to ignore that. "Julie," she begged, "I'm sorry about what I said that day."

"What did she say?" "Hey, Julie, tell us!" "Did she *swear*?" "Was it *awful*?" "Must of been something only a *wop* could think of!"

Rennie got hot all over. All thoughts of kindness vanished. *"You* leave *me* alone!" What was the use? It was good she'd buried the bracelet! It was good she'd been mean. She started off to look for her friends.

"Where do you think you're going, rotten wop?" Someone pulled at her sweater. It was the big white one. Rick's.

"Stop it!" she hollered. "You'll rip my sweater!"

"Ahhh!" "Poor Rennie!" "Haven't you got clothes your own size?" The kids were following her, prancing, almost pouncing, surrounding her, keeping in front, behind, next to her. She had no space to move.

"Stop!" she hollered again. She was getting hotter. She was sweating.

"Hennie Rennie, without a penny!" "Ragged Rennie!" "Ah! Don't rip her sweater! It's all she's got!" they mocked. "Hennie Rennie without a penny!"

"Stop it! It's my brother's sweater! He lets me wear it 'cause I like it!" Rennie searched around for someone she knew. She spotted Julie watching. Julie had a troubled look in her eye and Rennie called to her, "Julie! Tell them!"

Julie said nothing. The others kept teasing. They pushed Rennie from every side so there was nowhere to go. Someone pulled her sweater again. "Your father's a traitor! They shoot traitors!" She couldn't stand it. She swung out her arm! Someone's nose started to bleed!

The next thing she knew, a nun towered over her —black, mean. "Rennie Trani, this way!" she ordered, turning Rennie toward the school and poking her between the shoulders with her classroom pointer. "To the office!"

Rennie cringed and walked in helplessly. It would do no good to explain if the nun didn't already understand. She stood in the office without a word, looking straight ahead, breathing hard. At the nun's command, she held out the palm of her hand.

I am a powerful queen and no witch can hurt me.

The strap was slammed down upon her two sharp times. Pain screeched up her arm like fire and her dream vanished. Her whole body tightened into a knot, but she didn't cry. She clamped her teeth together. She glowered and didn't say another word all day.

After school she couldn't face the garden or Mama or any of her friends. Instead, she walked around downtown, one, two, three times. Finally, she stopped outside the chain link fence of the steel mill. Down the hill was its prison-like wall, nearly a mile wide, she thought, blocking the whole harbour. Its pipes were spitting their horrible smoke. It curled over the town like an eerie red devil. Up and down the street were demons of all kinds. There were miners coming home like black gremlins from underground. Slabs of cracked sidewalk pierced the air like tiny volcanoes. There were ragged dogs and wild kids howling and running in front of people.

The whole town was ugly.

She picked up a rock and hurled it at the fence. Clang! It fell back with a thud. She threw another and another and another with more force every time. Clang! CLANG! *CLANG!*

Now she could face people.

She went to the sparkling bakery that was missing her papa, but where many friends would be. Inside, people greeted her pleasantly and went about their talk as though nothing had happened. Rennie pulled up a stool and sat behind the far edge of the counter. She rested her chin in her good hand and stared into space. The noises about her were pleasant ones, a lot like on the day that the miners came bursting in.

This time, it was Mrs. McLean and Julie who came. They came quietly. Mrs. McLean looked shy, though she wore fresh lipstick as if it were a special occasion. Julie was behind her with a scowl on her face. The whole room fell quiet as the door eased shut. Rennie sat up and clutched her hands in her lap.

Mrs. McLean glanced uncomfortably at the people she'd barely spoken to since June. There was a new look on her face: sorrow. She said, "Caterina . . . "

Suddenly, Mama's eyes lit up and she stepped foward with her hands out. She took Mrs. McLean's hand between her own two and said, "So wonderful it is to have you here! I can help you? Yes?" She was smiling and excited. Rennie watched her in amazement, though it was Mama's true welcoming self.

Mrs. McLean was quite surprised, but she relaxed immediately. She pulled her hand away and held onto it loosely. "I — I've only come to apologize," she said. "About my husband, I mean. He had no right to try to hurt you."

Mama looked at her steadily. "Yes," she said, "but it was all right in the end."

"Thanks to Rennie, I understand." Mrs. McLean looked over at Rennie who had been hoping she wouldn't be seen.

"Julie has an apology for you, Rennie," she said. She put her hand on Julie's shoulder and pushed her forward slightly. Julie glanced up at Rennie and then looked at the floor.

"I should have helped you today," she said sullenly. "You didn't deserve the strap. I could have told what really happened."

She hadn't looked at Rennie once while she spoke. She'd only said it because she'd been forced. If Rennie had a strap, she would . . .

No. She wouldn't.

"How come you didn't?" she asked peacefully.

Julie just shrugged.

Mama was looking tense. At this moment of silence, she rushed over to Rennie and turned up her hands. She took the one with harsh red welts and cupped it between her own tenderly.

"What happened?" she asked. This time Rennie shrugged and Mrs. McLean explained.

"Julie says the children were teasing Rennie about Rick's sweater. They called her some terrible names and said, . . . " she paused for a long time, " . . . they said her father would be shot."

There was a gasp that went around the room. Mrs. McLean went on, "Rennie couldn't stand it and she hit somebody."

Rennie was watching Julie who was still looking at the floor. Julie wasn't sorry at all.

"We understand how Rennie feels about the sweater, too," said Mrs. McLean. "Julie loves Tom's I.D. bracelet just as much, but she lost it in the beginning of the summer. She misses it terribly."

Everyone was listening intently. Mama had her hand on Rennie's shoulder and after a moment, she said thank you to Mrs. McLean. She went and put two doughnuts in a bag and walked over to Julie. "For you and your mama," she offered, handing them over.

Julie took them but her mother took them from her. "No," she frowned at her daughter. "We don't deserve them just yet. Thank you anyway." She put the doughnuts on the counter and went home with Julie.

The bakery came alive with chatter. "I think now there is hope," said Mrs. Hobinsky. "Things will get better."

Later that evening Mama sat with Rennie at the kitchen table. She had a soft yet stern look that gave Rennie a twinge of fear. She asked, "Do you know anything about the bracelet?"

Rennie's eyes shot to the floor. Julie's words crowded her head. *Tom's braver than Rick; You're a rotten Italian and we all hate you; Don't be stupid; I'll pray your father never comes home.* Rennie had tried to be friendly and yet Julie hadn't helped her that afternoon or been sorry about it. Rennie wanted to scream out all the anger inside her.

She held her trembling jaw tight, but before she knew it, she looked at Mama for one quick minute and lied, "No." She looked down.

"I remember seeing you with it."

"But I gave it back."

"Then why aren't you looking at me?"

Rennie looked up. Was that doubt in Mama's eyes? "I gave it back," she said. The horror of the lie turned her stomach to rock. Where had kindness and bravery gone?

"All right," said Mama.

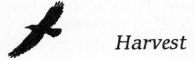

Harvest

Papa gave lickings for lies. Rennie shivered thinking of him standing over her, big and loud, the tyrant king. Now, how could he be proud of her? She had failed to make people like her family better. She'd been mean more than once. She had a stolen bracelet — almost stolen. She had lied about it even after she knew it was up to her to be good.

But she'd made the garden live beautifully. If only Papa could see it.

It was September and winemaking time. If only Papa could be home for that, but since he wasn't, they were skipping it. They didn't have the money to send for grapes, anyway. Rennie was sorry. She liked grape stomping.

Breadmaking wasn't so bad, either. She wanted Papa to watch her do it. And she wanted him to call her a porcupine out loud. When he did that, it made her grumpiness seem not so bad.

She wanted Papa to hear about all her troubles and hard work. He would tell her that she was braver and smarter and kinder than she had been in June.

I need Papa, she said to herself over and over. And if he punishes me, it will be worth it just to have him home.

At school they showed a film about the war. Row after row, the children craned their necks, eyes glued ahead.

The big square screen loomed above them. Music cheered. The announcer's voice filled the room. "Valiantly our boys will meet the enemy. We are ready for Hitler's army!" In black and white, parades of German soldiers thrust stiff legs forward —tin men come alive. "We must stop the march of evil forces," boomed the voice. "We must pray for our brave boys who have gone to fight. We must break the armies who would control the world."

Outside there was bragging about older brothers who'd joined up. Julie was the worst, sticking her nose in the air. "My brother, Tom, was one of the first ones. We're so proud of him. Daddy says there isn't a better thing a boy could do."

Giorgio spoke up with vehemence. "Does your brother know what they've done to my father, and Rennie's? They hate Hitler, too, but now my father can't work in the mine. And Rennie's got arrested! Just because they're Italian! They do the same good work that everyone else does. My father says he'd be ashamed to be a Canadian soldier because of what they've done to us!"

Julie eyes flamed with passion. "My brother's good! He would never hurt good people!"

Rennie could almost feel Papa's protective arms around her, but Julie's eyes were powerful. Rennie kept her voice low. "What did my father ever do bad?" She scanned the other children's faces. They had called her father a traitor. But Giorgio's speech seemed to have turned them silent.

"I don't know!" Julie shouted at Rennie. "It's not my brother's fault. He didn't arrest your father! Maybe he doesn't even know about it!" She was very upset. The kids were silent, looking at her, and waiting for what Giorgio would say next.

"Maybe you should tell him, then." Giorgio didn't shout it. He walked away with his shoulders slumped.

Julie started crying broken-heartedly. The other kids wandered off. Rennie's fear fell away and a lump came to her throat. This was still Julie who loved her brother.

Rennie swallowed the lump. Softly, she said, "Tom is good. I know it's not his fault. It's just — soldiers. War."

Julie sniffled hard and wiped at her eyes. "You're right, you know. Tom's gonna die because I lost his bracelet. I can't keep him safe anymore."

Why hadn't Rennie thought of *that* before? She took a deep breath and then let it out. "You'll find it, Julie. I know you will." Luckily the bell rang then, and nothing else had to be said.

Now there was only one thing Rennie could think of.

That afternoon she looked over the rows of thick green tomato plants. They had grown above her head and were covered with round red fruits — hundreds of them — that needed canning for winter. She held a pail in one hand and began picking, placing them gently on top of each other so as not to bruise them.

Papa, I'm learning to be good. I really am.

It didn't take much thinking. Just wrap your fingers around a fruit, without squeezing, and carefully twist it off. She barely had to watch what she was doing. Instead, she kept glancing toward the corner where the bracelet was. How could she? Julie would be so angry to discover where it had been. But, suppose Rick's sweater had disappeared? Suppose Rennie didn't have the tomatoes to bring Papa back?

She took a long, hard swallow. Then, she looked toward the windows of the house. Was anyone watching? No. She placed the pail on the ground.

She was terribly jittery. She would have to be fast, because if she got caught, there would be trouble.

She had to risk it. She had to set things right and let Julie know she understood her hatred and her sadness.

She moved through the tall plants — luckily they could hide her — and hurried to the weed. She bent to the ground and grabbed its stalk. She pulled with all her might. The roots came out and she threw the weed to the ground. Down on her hands and knees, she started digging. Dirt was caking under her nails. Then, Robbie came from around the corner of the house! Rennie jumped up!

"What do we have to do in the garden?" Robbie asked.

"Never mind, I'll do it myself. I'm used to it."

"Mama told me I had to help more, so I will."

Fine time to be good. She controlled her fear and anger. She told him to pick tomatoes. "But you're not near the tomatoes," he pointed out.

"I'm coming. Look, I've got a whole pail of them."

He shrugged and set to work, but his impatience grew. In a minute he was up, wandering around the edge of the garden looking for worms or slugs or anything more interesting than tomatoes.

Rennie prickled everywhere, but she kept quiet.

"Oooh, look at this one. Fat!" He knelt by the torn up weed and held up a thick earthworm. "Maybe there are more down there."

"Robbie! Tomatoes! Supper's almost ready!"

"Wait! How come this is dug up? You were digging it, weren't you? I bet your buried treasure's down there."

Toad! she screamed inside herself. "I knew you didn't really want to help," but Robbie's mind was on the hole. He lifted out huge piles of dirt. She was scared. She felt stabbed all over, as if her quills had turned toward her.

In a few moments, Robbie shouted, "Hey! Look at this!"

Her heart skipped a beat, but he was too fast for her, charging into the house, showing it off. She didn't know whether to go after him or to run away.

But Mama was at the back door instantly. "Renata!" she ordered, "get in here!" It was the first time she'd raised her voice to Rennie since Papa had gone.

Rennie hurried in with explanations falling off her tongue, "But, Julie was so mean to me! I had to bury it! But I was gonna take it back in the morning! I forgot about it! I! . . . "

With the switch in her hand, Mama pointed toward the stairs. *"Straight to your room, "* came her furious words.

"Oh, please don't! I'll take it to Julie right now! I'll say I'm sorry a hundred times! I *am* sorry! I shouldn't have been mean just because she was. That's what makes wars!"

Heavily, Mama sat down. She was shaking with anger and — something else. Her eyes were twisted with pain. Rennie couldn't turn away. "Renata, you have hurt Julia all summer! *And you lied!"*

"I couldn't help it," Rennie broke into sobs.

For a long moment, Mama said nothing, then she reached out her arms. "Come here," she whispered. Rennie seemed to melt right into her, Mama's arms were so warm around her. "It'll be all right. You can go to Julia's after supper."

The Gift

The words "Thomas McLean" shone up at Rennie. Those words on that bracelet had caused so much unhappiness. Now, as she washed away the soil under the faucet, beads of water danced on them.

It seemed to mean that something good would happen, but Rennie wasn't feeling sparkly. There was no telling what Julie would say, or Mr. or Mrs. McLean, for that matter.

She'd already had enough good luck, having escaped a licking.

But maybe that wasn't luck. Maybe that was Mama. Forgiving.

She polished the bracelet with a towel and placed it in the pocket of Rick's sweater. She stuck her hands in deeply for warmth, though the evening wasn't cold, and stepped into the clear night's air. One hand clutched the bracelet, the other held onto the inside of the sweater.

Very slowly, she walked down the street trying to pick out her words.

Maxie called, "Hi, Rennie." She was skating down her walk as Rennie passed. She slid to a stop. "How's your father?"

Maxie had a look of real interest on her face. "Why?" Rennie asked.

"He says he's OK, but he misses us," Rennie answered nicely. She was having trouble understanding why Maxie wanted to know.

"Sometimes my father talks about him. He didn't want to arrest him. He was only doing his job."

"Oh." It didn't make any sense. "It's because of your father that I stopped in front of you that day. I guess I shouldn't be mad at *you*."

"That's OK," Maxie got a little more excited then and leaned close to Rennie. She spoke almost in a whisper. "Hey, Rennie, I have a secret for you. But you can't tell anyone, especially not your mother. In case it doesn't turn out right. Daddy will kill me if he finds out I told."

"What?" Rennie held her breath.

"They called up Daddy the other day and asked about the Italians he arrested. He told them he thought your father was a fine, fine person. He'd never do anything wrong." Maxie's face was bright with happiness. How come Rennie didn't feel the same?

"So?"

"It means they might send your father home!"

"Oh!" Joy erupted on Rennie's face. "For real?"

"*Maybe*, " Maxie emphasized.

Rennie's heart was pounding. She skipped along toward Julie's house. Things would be all right!

Julie was sitting on her front porch playing with her cat. It probably meant Rennie wouldn't have to see Julie's parents, but she felt so good, she didn't care.

The low evening sun glanced off the side of Julie's face. She kept her eyes on the cat. Was she pretending she didn't know Rennie was there? Suddenly Rennie's stomach swarmed with butterflies. She made herself brave and stopped at the end of Julie's walk. Julie looked up because she had to. "What do you want?" she asked, finally.

Everything turned cold: the sweat on Rennie's hand; the silver metal of the bracelet; the sound of Julie's voice.

Without a word, Rennie held out the bracelet.

Julie nearly dropped her cat. She jumped up. *"You* had it!" she accused.

"I'm sorry. I'm sorry, I'm sorry, I'm sorry!" The words poured out of Rennie, nearly a hundred times.

Julie's accusing look turned to joy. She grabbed the bracelet and brought it to her lips, turning it around and around, kissing it. It made Rennie smile, but in a minute, Julie stopped and gave Rennie a look like fire.

"You stole it!"

"No, I didn't. It fell into my pocket. You had it on the edge of your desk. Remember? And when you grabbed your sweater, you must have knocked it off."

"No, I don't remember!" Julie insisted, "and why didn't you give it back?"

"I tried to but you wouldn't talk to me! You told me I was rotten. You told me you hated me." She paused. The power of her words calmed her voice to sadness. "And your father said the Italians should kill each other, and, and *I* hated *you.*"

The cat came and nuzzled against Julie's ankle. She sat down on the grass to cuddle it. She let her long blond hair fall around the animal and didn't say anything.

There was still a chance they might be friends. "But I know how much you need it so your brother won't get killed." Rennie waited, thinking about her own crop of short hair and how different she was from Julie. They used to enjoy being different. Now Julie kept nuzzling her cat. Rennie tightened her sweater around herself and turned to go.

She was down the end of the street and around the corner when Julie caught up with her, out of breath. She thrust a brown paper bag at Rennie.

"Here!"

It was the bottle of wine that Papa had given Mr. McLean. Rennie hugged it to her chest in terrible sadness.

Julie said, "My father doesn't want it."

"But it was a gift!"

"You said you didn't want him to have it, either. Remember?"

Her eyes are huge — round and flat — like blue ice. Her hair is stretched out — ugly yellow — like a thousand whiskery ropes. I'm a fire. I can melt and burn all that.

She could push Julie onto her bottom and make the pain fly through her!

For a few minutes longer she let Julie glare at her while she remembered everything. Most especially, she remembered what she wanted — but was she brave enough?

Yes, she was.

"I know why you won't forgive me, but if you change your mind someday, I'll be your friend again." There. She could breathe.

Julie's eyes turned surprised, then calm. She gave a very tiny, uncertain shrug before she walked away.

Rennie walked to the bakery and stuck her nose against its window, peering inside. The picture of that terrible afternoon when Papa was arrested came back to her: the policeman pulling the pictures from the wall; Papa, with his frightened look, caressing her hair, "*Ti amo*, Renata."

"*Ti amo*, Papa," she whispered, tears rolling down her cheeks.

She walked home. What would she do with the wine? She could never hurt Papa's feelings by letting him see it.

She buried it in the bracelet hole. As she packed the soil tightly over it and stood up to brush the dirt from her hands, she said out loud, "That's the end of all the badness in me."

She went around to her special plant. She hadn't been able to bear pulling off its tomatoes and they still hung all over it, round and red and bright. It was as tall as Rick and as welcoming as Mama. She sat in the dirt and looked up at it. "Please, please, bring home my papa." She put her head in her hands and cried. After a long time, there were no tears left. She looked up at the plant again. Feeling a little brighter, she stood up and turned toward the house.

There, standing by the corner of the house, was a figure, kind of short and fat and jaunty. A small suitcase sat on the ground and his arms reached out.

"Papa!" Rennie shouted with joy.

"Renata!"

They ran and fell into each other tightly. "Where are those quills?" Papa joked through eyes full of wetness.

"I buried them, Papa."

They hugged again, without words.

Epilogue

What happened to Rennie's father happened to approximately 700 Italian Canadian men and three Italian Canadian women in the summer of 1940. By June 12, 500 of these people had already been arrested. They came primarily from Ontario and Quebec, with a handful from Cape Breton, Nova Scotia. They were innocent people whose "crime" was their Italian heritage.

As *The Lie That Had To Be* indicates, some of the internees began to trickle home, without any notice to their families, within a few months after their arrest. Most, however, were detained for a much longer time. A great many were released in the winter of 1942 with a change in the Canadian Minister of Justice. A few were still in custody when Italy surrendered to the allied forces in September, 1943.

Aside from losing their freedom and contacts with their families, many of these people lost their businesses. And of course, their families suffered terribly.

AGMV Marquis

MEMBER OF SCABRINI MEDIA

Quebec, Canada
2001